Praise for *The Kind I'm Likely to Get*

"*The Kind I'm Likely to Get* is made u[...] these pieces form a cohesive work. The characters are all linked by the same basic yearning—whether they are children hiding from their mother in the woods, lonely lovers in launderettes, men wearing red dresses drinking mouthfuls of ash, or drunken couples falling through windows. They are ordinary people who reveal, through piercing obvservations born from resignation and self-deprecating humor, an off-kilter desire to lead lives that are beyond the ordinary. The book is full of paths not followed, actions not taken, desires unfufilled, and lovers not pursued. There is an edgy calmness to the writing that always seems ready to crack and bleed real blood. On closer inspection, the characters in this book are like grenades without pins: One has the unnerving sense that each story ceases moments before the explosion."
—EMER MARTIN, author of *Breakfast in Babylon* and *More Bread or I'll Appear*

"There is a keen, self-regarding wit as well as a good deal of pain in Ken Foster's collection of savvy, beautifully turned stories. Every detail is perfectly chosen to render the disorienting urban scenes in which his characters, mostly young and fragile, search for connection in random events and odd encounters. Foster's voice is steady, at times the essence of cool, but he is not afraid to contemplate the lessons of his difficult, often heartbreaking journey."
—MAUREEN HOWARD, author of *A Lover's Almanac*

"Wonderful, just short of too hip . . . as rueful as it is dead on."
—*The Village Voice*

"Foster's clean, spare prose seems ready for the Big Leagues."
—*Wired*

Praise for *The KGB Bar Reader*

"It's brutally quick, the way this happens, this falling in love with a writer's style. Part of the thrill . . . is realizing that there are other oddballs walking around out there, who look every bit as normal as you do, and that some of them know how to write. The best of these stories are too distinctive to suggest any trends, I'm happy to say. . . . They send you in search of other works by these writers."
—DAPHNE MERKIN in *The New Yorker*

"The *Reader* provides a kind of instant photograph of the present generation of writers: risk-taking, inventive, and breathtakingly deft at the art of revelation. These stories are a curtain drawn aside so we, the readers, can stare into hearts like locked rooms. . . . From the homely and the tender to the bizarre and nerve-flaying . . . *The KGB Bar Reader* covers a travelogue's range of settings, while exhibiting styles that range from the lyrically elegiac, to the laconic, to the most surreal of prose imaginings. . . . You could do worse things with $14 than spend it on a collection of this caliber. You could do few things better."
—*The Austin Chronicle*

"Perfect for a quick hit of contemporary lit."
—*Time Out New York*

"A gem . . . unforgettable . . . a collection of jarring stories that, whether fact or fiction, all appealed to Ken Foster's sharp ear."
—*Paper*

"The *Reader* spans literary canyons, cutting a path that links celebrities with struggling unknowns. . . . beguiling . . . mesmerizing . . . The texture of each selection is so unlike the one before that even the weaker entries don't detract from the satisfying balance of the book as a whole."
—*The Village Voice*

the kind i'm likely to get

by the same author

The KGB Bar Reader (editor)

the kind i'm likely to get

ken foster

a collection

Quill
William Morrow
New York

Copyright © 1999 by Ken Foster

"What Do I Do" written by Sam Phillips, © 1988
Eden Bridge Music (ASCAP). Administered by Bug Music.
All rights reserved. Used by permission.

Some of these stories were originally published, in a slightly different form, in *Bomb, Cups, The KGB Bar Reader,* and *Plazm.*

It is the policy of William Morrow and Company, Inc., and its imprints and affiliates, recognizing the importance of preserving what has been written, to print the books we publish on acid-free paper, and we exert our best efforts to that end.

Library of Congress Cataloging-in-Publication Data

Foster, Ken.
    The kind I'm likely to get : a collection / Ken Foster.
      p. cm.
    ISBN 0-688-16980-5
    1. United States—Social life and customs—20th century—Fiction.
  I. Title.
  PS3556.07598K5 1999
  813'.54—dc21
                                        99-11175
                                           CIP

Printed in the United States of America

First Edition

1 2 3 4 5 6 7 8 9 10

BOOK DESIGN BY LEAH CARLSON-STANISIC

www.williammorrow.com

sequence

If I set you on fire,

will you keep me warm?

—sam phillips

My mother is lighting another cigarette from the stove. She holds her hair back with one hand, to keep it from the flame. There are no lights on in the kitchen, so all I can see is her face and the sides of her head glowing as she bends over the flame. I'm sitting on the couch in the next room, watching through the open door. My little sister is asleep next to me. It's past her bedtime, but my mother hasn't bothered to put her to bed. Mom's just been sitting in the dark at the kitchen table, smoking. She hasn't said a word since I told her, just after dinner, "There's fleas in the carpet again."

"Shit," was all she said.

She finishes the pack and just sits in the dark for a few minutes.

"Wake your sister up," she says. "Put your coats and boots on. We're going for a ride."

"It's late," I say.

"That's okay," she says. "Go on."

So I help Jennifer on with her coat and boots. Her boots are secondhand and a little too big, and the rubber heel of one of them is hanging loose and hard to walk on.

"I'm tired," Jennifer says. "Can't I stay here?"

"It won't be long," I tell her. "We're just going to get cigarettes."

In the car, none of us say much. It's like we're all there just to get the job done. It's no family outing. I can see my mother's face glowing green from the dashboard light and our headlights shining on the empty road in front of us. "You don't know, do you?" my mother says. "You don't know what it's like."

I'm not sure what she's talking about, so I don't say anything. Jennifer's lying on the seat next to me, with her head on my lap. My fingers are playing with the fur inside the hood of her coat. The fur is soft but lumpy, from too many washes. In the distance I can see the mountains lying like sleeping bodies draped over with blankets and the lights of a service station we approach and pass.

The lights that run along the highway are far apart but close enough together to imagine they're a string of lights, like Christmastime, like the lanterns that line the way to church on Christmas Eve, made of brown paper bags with candles and dirt in the bottom to keep them in place. Sometimes people forget to put them out in their yards and there's suddenly a dark patch unexpectedly, but never enough that you can't see where the lights pick up again. And it's like the candles in the church when we stayed with Grandpa and he'd let Jennifer and me down to the basement after, to drink the little glasses of leftover grape juice and eat the little squares of bread cut like dice. Some days we'd walk the railroad tracks collecting things: spikes, arrowheads from the woods, and from the telephone poles green glass insulators like Coke bottles. Insulators were the best.

"Aren't we going for cigarettes?" I ask.

My mother doesn't answer. She just keeps driving, past the railroad tracks of the train we always hear in the distance.

"We going for a train ride?" I ask. I know it can't be true, but she's always promising one day we will.

At nights sometimes in my mother's house, after everyone's asleep, I go into the kitchen, to the drawer next to the fridge, and reach into where she keeps the birthday candles. She pulls them off the cake as soon as we blow them out. She saves them for the next time. Six for Jennifer's birthday and then six and six again for me. "I'm too old for candles," she says. At night sometimes I stand in the light from the fridge, and I hold the candles in my hand. I run my fingers along the edges, along the smooth trails of melted wax. I hold them in my hand. They mean something good will happen.

Then, once we've passed what used to be the horizon and passed it another time again, my mother pulls the car over to the side of the road and gets out. There are trees thick on either side and curving in front and behind so it's hard to have any idea where we are. We might as well be in any dark room right now. The coatroom at school, with the doors closed.

"I hope you were paying attention," Mom says through the open door. She nods her head and says, "You gotta learn you can't depend on me to always take care of things." Her right arm is stiff at an angle from her body, and she's breathing slow and easy. It's like she's smoking, but without the cigarette. "Come on now. Get out of the car."

I nudge Jennifer and help her out of the car. She's uneasy on her feet from being so tired and not knowing where she is and the broken heel and all. I follow her out and take her hand and lead her to the gravel next to the road.

"I'm gonna head home now," Mom says. "And I want you two to follow me on foot. And I want you to think about things, you two."

My mother gets back in the car and turns it around, catching us for a second in the headlights, then heads off, beyond the curve. Out of sight. The wind blows past us and follows her car down the road.

It takes a minute for my eyes to adjust. I look up past the trees to the narrow strip of light. The midnight sky looks light next to the darkness. Jennifer's holding on to my leg. I can feel her body against me, but I can't tell if it's 'cause she's cold or she's crying. I lift her up, and she rests her head against my shoulder. I don't know what to tell her. I just walk back the way my mother left.

We keep stopping so I can put Jennifer down, and we rest. Sometimes I can get her to walk a ways, but the heel on her boot keeps making her trip and I'm afraid she'll twist her ankle. Jennifer's nose is running, but we don't have any Kleenexes so I tell her it's okay to use her sleeve. When one gets too dirty, she switches to the other.

We don't talk much. I wonder if this is what my mother had in mind.

Jennifer bends over and picks up a pinecone, and then another.

"What are you collecting pinecones for?" I ask.

"I don't know," Jennifer says.

I pick Jennifer up again, and we walk past another bend in the road. The fur of her hood rubs against my cheek, and I pull her close to get warm. We're heading for a little bridge that crosses a stream up ahead. I don't remember passing it on the way out, but then I wasn't paying attention.

When we get up to the bridge, we each take a pinecone and throw it over the side, then we run to the opposite side to see whose will come out first. The ripples of the water are just different shades of dark, and the deep blue of the sky and a little ripple of white from the moon. Our pinecones come out, sort of circling each other in the current. We watch them until they pass through the moon.

"When are we going to be done?" Jennifer asks.

"It just takes a lot longer when you walk," I tell her. I don't recognize anything at all. We stop and sit down as long as we can, so I can try to figure out what to do. I look up at the sky. Once, my mother showed me the Big Dipper and the Little Dipper and some people up in the sky if you connect the dots, but I don't remember. I guess you can make anything out of the stars if you know where to draw the lines.

There are lights coming down the road, so I grab Jennifer and run into the woods. Mom always says that's what to do when a car comes, even in daylight. They'll drag you right in. I turn around as the car stops by the side of the road. Jennifer's got her head over my shoulder, facing back into the woods, so she doesn't see that it's our mother's car. And I don't tell her. I just sit quiet and watch my mother get out of the car. She stands looking out over the hood, the car light shining up at her, making shadows on her face. She has a flashlight in one hand and a lit cigarette in the other. The orange tip of the cigarette moves from her side to her mouth while she shines the flashlight into the woods. Short clouds of smoke rise from her mouth and disappear just above her head, like smoke signals from Indians. She raises the hand with the cigarette and wipes the corner of her eye with the tips of her fingers. I think I see the orange tip of her cigarette begin to burn the ends of her hair. The flashlight light bounces between the trees but never makes it past them. The light doesn't hit Jennifer and me. My mother gets back in the car and drives away slow.

"Are they after us?" Jennifer asks.

"Yeah," I say. Then I lie to her. I tell her, "But we're okay."

We can hear the sound of water dripping, of a deer running home between the trees late at night, and if we are very quiet, when Jennifer is sleeping, sometimes I think I hear the sound of tires on the road, of our mother returning again, or driving away in the distance.

indelible

The only other person in the Laundromat, a blond woman in her twenties, stood at the folding table across from John. He tried not to notice her. He sat resting his right foot on his left knee, his chin propped up by both hands. The buckles of his black leather jacket dangled over the edge of the bench, the lace of one Doc Marten untied. He was clearly succeeding in his attempt to look forlorn, but the woman didn't seem to care.

John noticed that the woman's underwear alternated in colors as she folded it and popped it into her black gym bag. Pink, light blue, yellow, light green. Easter colors, he thought. He considered telling her this, but lately, whenever he met a woman he wanted to talk to, his mind flashed forward to the inevitable moment when they would no longer be speaking to each other. So instead of speaking to her, he stared into the washing machine in front of him and watched as the suds turned from white to gray to charcoal black. He thought he might begin to cry.

He'd been testing the colorfastness of a new design he'd silk-screened onto a T-shirt. The ink he'd used had been labeled "indelible" on the front of the tube, but "water soluble" in smaller letters on the back. He wondered how anything could be both simultaneously. But first he wanted to perfect his original, most personal design: a simple doodle of a locomotive with cockroach legs. He had been leaving it as a tag since college. He tagged everything with it: buildings, street signs, bathroom walls, cocktail napkins, the ankles of women while they slept.

John thought maybe he could make some money with it, because people were always asking him what it meant. On good days it was a cockroach turning into a locomotive, on bad days it was a locomotive turning into a cockroach, but most days it was just a locomotive with cockroach legs and when people asked what it meant, John just rolled his eyes in a way that made them feel stupid for asking.

As he watched his latest failure pass into the final rinse, he considered his options. It was nearly summer, and outside the open door of the Laundromat, people were walking by in shorts and T-shirts and less. It seemed the entire neighborhood was becoming a clothing-optional society. The Laundromat was set down from the sidewalk by a short flight of stairs and lit by only a few bare bulbs, so the outside world seemed unnaturally bright. He watched the disembodied legs as they marched by the window—women in shorts, miniskirts, some in thigh-high boots. Perhaps it was time for a change. Perhaps he should retire the black leather jacket, or at least stop wearing it to the beach. Maybe it was time to stop dying his hair. It was possible he'd feel better if he went home and shaved his head. But what he really wanted to do was talk to Mary.

John glanced back at the woman with the Easter-colored underwear.

Mary had left behind a small drawer full of black underwear when she packed up her car and took off across the country, promising to send postcards from the road. She and John had been friends for a long time, meaning that they hung out in the same crowd but rarely spoke to each other. They ended up getting together unexpectedly at a New Year's party a year and a half ago. It was a small party, and at one point everyone was gathered around exchanging stories about the fucked-up couples they knew. Mary said, "What I don't understand is why any of you are surprised. I mean, how many couples do you know who aren't fucked up in some way?" John turned to her and said, "We're not fucked up." He meant it as a joke, but when he said it, he saw something soften behind her eyes and he thought it was possible he really did like her.

After the party he walked her back to her apartment, and she invited him in to hear stories about the strange people she met while temping. He ended up staying the night, not because he had been invited, but because he hadn't been asked yet to leave.

Later, after Mary packed her car and left town, John realized he was the kind of man who would sit up all night if there wasn't someone there to turn out the light and tell him it was time to sleep.

Now, when he sees people they both knew—people who were probably there at that New Year's party—he tells them, "Mary's doing really well," even though he hasn't heard a word from her in the months since she left. He imagines her living in New Mexico, in a little mud house she's built with her own hands. He sees her melting snow for water, living off sprouts and doing laundry by hand. Never mind the fact that when she lived in the city she filtered the water twice, sent out for pizza, and sent everything to the cleaner's, including her underwear. He always thought Mary had the capacity for unrecognizable change, and he's sure she's happy now. If she ever decided it was time to move on, she could just hose down her little mud house till there was nothing left and no one would ever know she had been there.

He remembered sitting in a café with Mary and speculating on the status of the other couples in the room. They had watched, at the next table, a boy and girl hold hands and exchange information on their ethnicities. "Does your mother speak *any* English?" the boy had asked. And just beyond them, a woman in an Anne Klein suit approached an apparently estranged friend who had been trying to ignore her. John and Mary watched as the women squealed and embraced. A few tables away, another couple sat in silence, the woman staring away from the man's gaze; he reached across the table and grabbed her jaw to pull her attention to him.

"I'm a cynic," Mary said then. "Lately I look back on all my relationships and it seems that they were all either extremely temporary or inextricably permanent."

John asked, "Which one am I?"

Mary thought for just a moment. "You," she said, "seem to fall somewhere in between."

It was on this very same date—an early one—that John told Mary the story of "Monkeys! Clowns! Circus!" He'd been trying to impress her by saying something clever and ironic, but nothing he came up with seemed to do the trick.

"You're not the first man to tell me that," Mary said to his final attempt.

"No," John said. "But I am the first man to ever say, 'Monkeys! Clowns! Circus!' " His eyes widened with each word, as if he was casting a maniacal spell.

"What?"

"Monkeys! Clowns! Circus!"

Mary shook her head. "I don't understand."

"Only my sister and I know what it really means," he said.

Mary looked down at her menu. "So what does it mean?"

John told her the story of how—maybe twenty years earlier—he and his older sister, Ginger, were playing one afternoon at the foot of her closet. While John pulled toys arbitrarily from the shelves, Ginger grabbed his hand and said, "Listen to me. I'm about to tell you something very important . . . because what I'm about to say is something we will remember for the rest of our lives."

John dropped Barbie and G.I. Joe to the floor, he was so struck by Ginger's serious tone. It seemed she was about to say something she'd been thinking over for a very long time.

"Monkeys, Clowns, Circus," she said. "Only you and I will know what it means."

John nodded, pretending, as usual, that he understood.

They kept the words to themselves, using them only on special occasions when nothing else would make sense. They would whisper the phrase in each other's ears during their parents' arguments or, when they were older, write the words on the bottom of a particularly melancholy letter. "It's over between me and Lynn," his sister once wrote. "Maybe I'm not a lesbian after all. Love, Ginger. Monkeys. Clowns. Circus."

John told Mary, "We should have something like that. Our own special code."

"Well," Mary had said, "okay . . ." She looked over the menu for inspiration. "How about . . . White Cheddar Cheese Burger Pizza."

"Great," John said, but he was disappointed. He'd been hoping for something a little more personal.

A few nights later, after dinner and a movie and some drinks downtown, John said to her, "You know what I'm in the mood for?"

"What?" Mary said, keeping her eyes on the DON'T WALK light blinking across the street. She was holding her latex jacket with one hand and smoking with the other. John loved watching her.

"I'm in the mood for some White Cheddar Cheese Burger Pizza," he said.

"Really?" Mary said. "This late? Aren't you still full from dinner?"

She hadn't even remembered.

John watched the girl in the Laundromat fold her shirts and place them carefully in the black bag. She ran her hands over her jeans and tossed them back in the dryer for another quarter's worth of heat. He turned back to his washer and his newest mistake entering the spin. He remembered the first time he had introduced Mary to Ginger. They met for drinks, and after two rounds Mary decided to go home early. "You guys can stay and do your brother-sister thing," she said. He worried that he hadn't paid enough attention to her.

Ginger said, "I just don't think she's a very nice person."

A small black bag sat abandoned beneath Mary's chair—one

of those nylon, all-terrain, floppy briefcases. "Are you sure it's hers?" Ginger asked when John grabbed it. "I mean, it looks like something a businessman would take with him into the jungle."

"No," John said. "It's hers. I'll give it to her when I meet her for breakfast in the morning."

As he carried the bag home, he grew curious about what might be inside. It seemed both heavy and empty, like there was a small weight hidden at the bottom. When he got back to his studio apartment, he carried the bag straight to the bathroom. He closed the bathroom door, as if for privacy, sat on the toilet, and carefully undid the zipper to the bag. He looked inside. There was a gun resting in its holster. A .357 Magnum. He saw the make indelibly engraved into the metal as he considered checking to see if the gun was loaded. But he got nervous and put it back in the bag instead, left the bathroom, and shut the door behind him, as if for protection. He called Ginger to ask what he should do.

Ginger said, "I don't like that woman."

"But what if she was planning to kill herself? What if I give it back to her and she shoots herself? But if I tell her I'm not giving it back, she'll know I looked inside."

"Maybe she's shooting heroin," Ginger said cheerfully. "Maybe she just carries it for protection when she goes to score her supply."

"No," John said. "If she was carrying it for protection, she'd keep it more available. She was planning on doing something with it. She had some kind of plan.'' He was always certain that Mary, unlike him, had some kind of plan.

When he met Mary in the morning, he held the bag up and oversmiled. ''I have your bag,'' he said.

''What are you talking about?'' Mary said. ''That's not my bag.''

Sitting in the Laundromat, watching the washing machine go through its final spin, John wondered if maybe that had been the attraction to Mary. That he thought she could carry a gun. That with her anything seemed possible, even if it wasn't.

The woman in the Laundromat was folding the last of her laundry and putting it away. John was sure he had never seen her before and wondered if their meeting might, therefore, be fate. Then he thought perhaps he *had* seen her before, in some type of commercial, but he couldn't remember which one. She looked up and caught John looking at her. He allowed himself the fantasy of her spread out across the folding table, modeling underwear for him. But in his fantasy, he imagined the underwear was black and the bra, like Mary's, unsnapped in the front. He looked back at his reflection in the glass window of the washing machine.

He thought back on his and Mary's decision to move in together, and how they had probably arrived at it more out of boredom than out of any sincere desire. In fact, he was certain now that it was out of desperation that Mary had moved in. She had been arguing with her roommates, he remembered, and had been spending more and more time at his place until finally it seemed to make more sense for her to bring all of her things over. Mary moved in on a Saturday in October, the first cold snap of the season. She emerged from a taxi wearing a strange oversized peacoat and carrying a suitcase in each hand. John grabbed the few boxes out of the trunk, and Mary pulled out three odd black tubes and carried them under her arms. He felt let down; he'd been expecting a truckload of curious objects, each with a mysterious history she might share. Instead, all she seemed to have were a few boxes of used books.

Later she showed him how the black tubes, when placed properly together, formed the frame for a small dining room table.

"It's held together by tension," she said. "Like everything else."

John was alarmed by how much time Mary spent at home. She stopped taking temp assignments, saying she was looking for something more permanent, but the Sunday *Times* was stacked unopened in the recyclables each week. John found himself getting less of his own work done. Every time he started drawing anything—a doodle of the locomotive with cockroach legs, a preliminary sketch for a mural with a circus theme—he found

Mary looking over his shoulder, asking, "But what does it mean?"

Meanwhile, Ginger seemed to be enjoying her single life, telling him at every opportunity, "I don't know why that woman is still in your apartment." To which John replied with a shrug, "Monkeys, Clowns, Circus."

In the end, in the final weeks, they were staying together because they thought briefly that she might be pregnant, neither of them wanting to confirm the situation because neither of them wanted to suggest what the other was already thinking: that this had all been an incredible mistake, that before it was too late, they would have to take steps to erase it. When she told him it wasn't true—that it *had* been a mistake, everything was fine—the first thing he said was "I guess we don't have to stay together anymore." He said it out loud, because he thought it was probably what she was thinking, too.

For several days they didn't speak to each other at all. He sat alone, wondering how anything so permanent could have been so temporary, and he found he liked the idea still of the two of them somehow being bound together. When he came home and found Mary packing, he almost said, "I'll go with you," before he realized she was leaving to get away from him.

If he knew where she was now, he might call information to get her number. He wouldn't talk to her, though. He just wanted to see if she would pick up, to know she was there.

．　．　．

John opened the washing machine and pulled out the wrinkled shirt. He stretched it across his lap. The locomotive with cockroach legs had turned into a gray cloud in the middle of the shirt. A man with homemade tattoos on his arms mopped up and down the aisles, pausing to remove sheets of lint from the dryers. John remembered someone—was it Mary or Ginger?—telling him that dust and lint are made mostly of human skin. He watched the man's tattooed arms—the ink blurred into his flesh—as he gathered the sheets of lint into a large ball and tossed it away.

The woman brushed by John with her small black gym bag. She paused for a moment and looked down at his lap.

She said, "You need to let it set first, before you can wash it."

John watched as she walked out into the street. His eyes followed her legs as they passed the window and disappeared. He looked back at the gray cloud resting in his lap and thought of a new design: a shirt that read WATER SOLUBLE in large letters as they walked toward you and INDELIBLE in smaller letters from the back, when they left you behind.

The men were all worried about their hemlines. They stood in groups discussing the merits of length, while the women stood in line for the phone, waiting to call out, or sat in groups around the men, occasionally giving advice, like how to walk in a narrow cut or how to avoid a run in sheer stockings.

But everything was fine at the Red Dress party. It was only later that things began to unravel.

I hadn't planned to attend. I've never enjoyed parties much and didn't have the right clothes, didn't like the idea of having to buy a dress for the sake of a party, a red dress being mandatory attire for things like this. Besides, I'd always felt men didn't look good in dresses, and I hadn't been out of the house in a while, except to work. I'd been busy with a little crying jag for the past couple of weeks, but I wasn't too worried, because it felt kind of good.

It wasn't until I curled myself up on the closet floor to think things through that I noticed the red cloth bleeding through between suits of gray flannel. It wasn't Anne's style at all. Sort of a mother-of-the-bride kind of thing. A red mother-of-the-bride kind of thing. It didn't surprise me that she had left it behind when she left me, but I was surprised it fit me. I remembered Anne as being a much smaller person.

It was still light out when I drove up the winding hillside road to the Doctor's house. None of us really knew the Doctor except Dan, who was giving the party. He had met the Doctor through another friend when he realized the guests would never fit in his own house. It was one of those parties where people invited friends who invited other people, so by the time I got there, I couldn't remember who had told me to come.

I parked my car along the road and walked barefoot through the yard. Only a few guests had arrived, and they were gathered on one of the balconies overlooking Portland. I looked up at the men and women standing in red dresses, the dresses rustling in the wind, framed against an overcast sky like leaves about to fall.

I had some trouble negotiating the lawn in a dress. It narrowed at the knees. The women began to point and laugh.

"Oh, you look lovely," they called.

I looked up to see if I knew them. I held my hand above my eyes to shield them from the sun behind the clouds. In red dresses, it was hard to tell anyone apart. It was hard to see if they might be friends of Anne's, the friends who told me when she left, "I'll never speak to you again." The friends who, I realized, had never said anything more to me than that.

Inside the house, everything was cream walls and pale wood floors. The furniture had been removed to make room for people who couldn't be trusted. A girl in a red dress sat on the stairs talking on a cellular phone to someone who was far away. I thought I'd always wanted to go to a party where people talked on cell phones, instead of to each other. It was like something from a movie.

On the balcony people gathered still, talking of the weather. A woman in a red dress turned to her husband and said, "This is why I moved here."

He said, "The weatherman says it's going to clear up."

I said, "That's what they've been saying, but every day is the same."

"Exactly," the woman said, and smiled.

I took a seat and watched as the guests rolled in. Red gowns, red skirts, red polka-dot spandex on a bodybuilder. One man wore a dark suit with a tiny doll's red dress pinned to his lapel. No one argued with him. From across the room, two women watched their husbands in red dresses. One of the women, wearing a red pillbox hat, said, "He looks better in that dress than I do." By the end of the night, when she was fruitlessly searching the red mass for her husband, we were calling her Jackie O.

People disappeared upstairs to stand in line at the bathrooms and return with new faces. Red lipstick, rouge, some with eyes rimmed in shadow.

It was in my bathroom, clearing out the makeup after Anne left, that I had planned how I would kill myself. I pictured myself standing before the mirror, a gun to my head, anxious to pull the trigger—if only I had one. The idea excited me, not because I wanted to die, but because I was capable of doing it. It was something I could do to make one day unlike any other. The possibility of watching my head burst in a red cloud in the mirror kept me going. I woke up each day to see if it would happen. But it didn't, and every day seemed like every other.

At the party, Joyce stood alone before the mirror, trying to cover the gray circles under her eyes—the signs that she wasn't really in remission. "I look like a raccoon," she said. She smiled at me and said, "I wasn't going to come. Ed was afraid people would think he'd beaten me."

"Why didn't he come with you?" I asked.

"He said any party where you have to wear a red dress is stupid." Joyce laughed. "Maybe he was just afraid."

"He probably should be," I said, and for an instant I thought I'd said *we* instead of *he*.

Joyce asked how I was doing.

"I'm fine," I said. "I'm getting better."

Joyce said we couldn't stay in the bathroom all night and maybe we should go back outside.

I said, "Only if we have to."

As we passed through the kitchen, I overheard two red-dressed women talking about Joyce.

"I'd never go out in her condition," one said, and the other, with a red feather boa wrapped around her neck, agreed. She said, "Looking for sympathy," and nodded. I wondered what they'd say about me when I was gone. Joyce seemed not to notice, and I wondered for a moment if they might actually be talking about me.

Joyce and I stepped out onto the balcony with drinks in our hands and looked down to the city below. The lights were masked by fog and drizzle. We could see the lights of neighboring windows shining through the narrow spaces between the trees.

I said, "It wouldn't be so bad if it would actually rain."

We stood quiet for a while, looking at nothing in particular. The lights from the warehouse district cast a pink hue in the sky.

I said, "It doesn't seem like anyone knows we're here."

We stood on the sidelines for the rest of the night, drinking and watching people talk about what a great idea the red dresses were.

"A great equalizer," someone said. "I feel as if I can talk to anyone."

When I wasn't looking, someone used my drink as an ashtray. I didn't notice until I had swallowed a cup of ash. The Doctor whose house we were in began to clean up around us, collecting the debris others had left behind. We watched as he circled us.

"I never even met him," I told Joyce.

She said, "Neither did I."

I didn't trust myself to drive home safely, and no one offered a ride. I began to walk back down the hill in my bare feet, the mist collecting in my dress. Carloads of red-dressed people passed me by without stopping. I stretched my arms out and let the air blow through me. Light caught in the fog, an orange glowing haze formed over the city, the wind picked up the leaves around me, and I thought, this feels good somehow: to be alive. I didn't notice the hem of the dress tearing a little with each clumsy step, red thread trailing the ground behind me.

Along the side of the Hawthorne Bridge, a single shoe was resting on its side. I wondered, how can that happen—that someone leaves a single shoe behind? I heard the crisp sound of tires slowing on wet pavement, the sound of a car door as it opened and closed, and tasted a leather glove as he reached around me to cover my mouth.

Of course, this is how it happens.

. . .

I'd been in the hospital for nearly a week before I understood the extent of my injuries. One of my ribs had punctured a lung. My jaw had been dislocated on the right side. My lips were cut in two places, and one eye swollen shut.

Other injuries were internal.

They sent a policewoman to ask me questions. Her first question was, "Had you been drinking?"

I shook my head. "Why?"

"Well, because . . . you were wearing a . . . a . . ."

"A red dress," I said.

"We're just trying to establish any motive."

"You're wearing pants," I said. "Have you been drinking?"

Friends came to visit, once it seemed clear I would make a full recovery. I was wearing one of those white hospital gowns that leave you exposed where you are most vulnerable.

I didn't rise to meet them.

They came in a group and wandered the room like manic tourists who had just arrived in a foreign country. They wore long beige coats kept buttoned from head to toe.

They pointed at familiar objects as if seeing them for the first time.

Look at the television!

You get cable?

How's the food?

Look at the view!

Have you met anyone interesting?

Finally someone asked how I was feeling.

I told them the only thing I thought they'd understand.

Fine, I said. Just fine.

No one pointed to the red dress that hung from the wardrobe in a plastic bag. Someone on staff had thought to have it dry-cleaned.

the circuit

Kevin has an unfortunate tendency to brood, which he says accounts for his traveling so much. He comes to Portland to tell stories of his life in New York, and in New York he tells everyone what things were like out West, how the people and places seem to run back and forth in an invisible circuit, but when he tells these stories in New York, people tend not to believe him. People in New York, he tells Susan, are trained to filter out hyperbole and thus assume a percentage of everything isn't true.

He and Susan are sitting in the lounge of a restaurant on NW 23rd, just a few blocks away from the coffee shop they both used to work in, until he left and went back to New York a year ago. She's arranged an evening for him now that he's back, a sort of whirlwind tour of the latest hangouts, because although nothing much has changed since he left, the places where things occur have altered, so she has to act as tour guide. As soon as his flight landed, he took the bus to Powell's Books and met her in the coffee shop. He saw her first, sitting with a magazine and half a cappuccino in a paper cup. Although most people wouldn't guess it, if you know where to look, you can tell she used to do print work, she used to model. In her eyes (if she's looking at you), in her smile (although one of her teeth is chipped), in her posture (but only when something makes her happy). Kevin thinks he could be in love with her, if only it would get him anywhere.

Sitting at a corner table in this restaurant, he thinks of telling her this, how there's a chance he might have some feelings. But now Susan's on a storytelling roll, and he decides it would be rude to interrupt.

She's sitting across the table with her beer hardly touched, a Dunhill Blue smoldering in the ashtray. She's riffing on the staff as they pass by, because she knows everything about them. Most nights she'd be working the floor alongside them, but with Kevin in town, she has the night off. She's taken him here as a first stop because she can rely on the service, she can count on her colleagues' slipping them a deal on drinks and hors d'oeuvres, and since most of the tales she has to tell revolve around the people she works with, it saves on verbal illustration. All she has to do is point and talk.

Susan is explaining how she and André decided to live together after splitting up, and how she's enjoying not being involved with anyone, although she and André still fool around occasionally.

"So you're not involved," Kevin says. "You just live together and have sex?"

Susan laughs smoke and sips her microbrew. A waitress stops

by, and Susan introduces her. Kevin immediately forgets her name. Once the waitress is out of earshot, Susan says, "You know, that's who he left me for. And then she and I ended up getting together for a while after she left him." Susan points to a waiter across the room, a tall blond surfer type. "I was with him a few nights ago," she says. Another waitress passes. "And she was with us."

Then she adds, "He really had no clue. What a waste of time that was."

"So what you're telling me is, you've had sex with everyone in the room."

"Except you."

Kevin remembers the time he stopped by her house after work one night and walked in on her and André having sex on the kitchen table, silhouetted in the blue moonlight from the window. After he left, he sat breathless in his car, uncertain of how long he'd stood in the doorway watching. Uncertain of whether or not they knew he was there. It might have been minutes or just a few seconds. It was always hard to tell. Time gets distorted in those moments.

Kevin tells her that in New York, people talk about sex more than they actually have it. "There isn't enough space," he says, and then he thinks about it and decides it's actually true. You spend so much time involuntarily on top of people during the day, sometimes the last thing you want is to be inside one of them at night. Of course, this suits Kevin just fine for now, because he moved to New York to be anonymous, rather than, like everyone else, to be famous. Even when he'd arrived in Portland a few years back, he'd done it hoping to get out of the loop he'd been in. He was looking for a way to derail, to disconnect. When he finally landed a job, it was at a ridiculous industrial-themed coffee shop called Coffee People, located on NW 23rd, which was the hip strip for both yuppies and slackers. Steel girders jutted up from the floor and out of the walls, for no apparent reason other than some architect's idea of cool aesthetic.

People sat Indian-style on the sidewalk up and down the street. The overeducated and underemployed bought one cappuccino after another while discussing what part of their bodies should be pierced next. As much as the crowd held a certain fascination for him, he never quite fit in. It was as if they could tell he had ambitions, even if he didn't know it himself. Overheard conversations inevitably included the words "I've been doing a lot of writing."

Susan was the manager then, and she liked Kevin because he was always saying the things she could never get away with as a manager. He was always arguing about how bitter things should be. He liked the perfect one-ounce shot, the orange crema blanketing the pitch-black coffee below. Single, double, triple. Wet or dry. People who knew what they wanted and how to ask for it. He hadn't counted on people asking for decaf, for special sweeteners to disguise the true essence of what they wanted.

He hadn't expected the requests for caramel fudge mochas or Mexican chocolate, or the tourists who asked, in advance, "Is the coffee bitter?"

"Well," he would tell them, "it is coffee."

Tourists would line up on weekends, safe inside the air-conditioned espresso shop, dusting pollen from their shoulders and anticipating a new experience, something to write home about. One in every group would order a double shot, their companions' eyes widening at their bravery.

Then, "Is that it? It's so small! That's all I get?"

"Do you want something else?"

"Well, I don't know," they would say, waiting for him to tell them what they wanted.

"Don't you have milk?" they would ask. "Can you put it in a cup of steamed milk?"

"A latte?"

"Yes. And chocolate. That's what I want."

"A mocha," he would tell them.

"I don't know," the customer would say with a shrug.

The decaf customers were the most unbearable. Decaf, Kevin thought, is the methadone of the coffee world and should be made available only at special clinics and by prescription. He wanted to post rules and expel the customers who wouldn't follow them. Customers who insisted that their table be wiped off before they sat down to leave their own mess behind. Customers who asked for water not because they were thirsty, but because they wanted to ask for something and not have to pay for it. He made these lists driving home from work every night.

Worse, he found the more he tried not to be involved, the more involved he became. He'd cover for Susan while she had sex with André in the back room. He tried to stay out of staff arguments. When Bruce harassed Kevin on his technique, shouting, "Always wipe your wand," from the bean section every time Kevin began frothing the milk, Kevin ignored it, but that only inspired Ron to defend him, so that eventually Ron and Bruce were at each other's throats over him. He spent time with Charity and realized too late that she was in love with him. But Susan was different. On breaks they'd go outside to watch as things passed by. They sat with the other regulars on the sidewalk, sharing cigarettes silently, chairs facing the street as if they were waiting for a parade that would never come.

Then, as summer approached, people began to disappear. Ron came out of the closet and moved to San Francisco, taking Charity with him. Bruce left for Seattle and an offer to join a band. Then Kevin and Susan were fired in a dispute over some money missing from the safe. Kevin left for New York again, thinking he might move back after a few months, but, as he tells Susan, "Once you move there, you never have enough money to leave again."

"Did I tell you Charity came back?" Susan asks. "She came twice actually. I was surprised at how good it was to see her again. She ended up hooking up with some corporate job, having an affair with the woman who hired her and her girlfriend. Swearing off men altogether. Which wasn't that surprising when I thought of it. Then, a few months later, she was back again. With a rich boyfriend from South Africa.''

''Which also wasn't very surprising, I guess.''

It was Charity they had suspected of stealing the money, because she was the kind of person you could imagine doing anything.

After drinks, Kevin and Susan wander the old neighborhood. They stop in to the coffee shop, which seems deserted to Kevin.

''No one hangs out in Northwest anymore,'' Susan explains. ''They're all over on Hawthorne now.''

It's true. There are only a few customers seated at the tables. Kevin and Susan watch their own replacements at work behind the counter. Kevin wonders if maybe they're even wearing the same aprons, maybe the coffee stains down the front were left by him. They seem too calm, too young; there's none of the frantic energy he remembers from when they were working there.

Kevin takes a stack of customer-comment cards. ''I'm going to fill them out with scathing comments,'' he says, though he knows the cards will still be stuffing his pockets when he gets back to New York. They head down the street, collecting cards from all the shops Kevin worked at one time or another. Then they head across the river to the restaurant where André is working, beneath the highway, in southeast Portland.

Already Kevin is thinking about how this will play back in New York, how he needs to find something funny to hang it on, a sardonic, bittersweet hook. They park beneath the overpass, which swoops and twists, Kevin thinks, like something out of Dr. Seuss. On the way in, Susan points to a pay phone on the corner where she and a friend performed a short scene for an independent film.

"We played lesbian lovers," she says. "It was in town for about a week. Even I didn't get to see it, but someone told me about it."

Ellen is hostessing. She used to work on 23rd, too. At the cigar and magazine shop down the street from Coffee People. She welcomes Kevin back with a big kiss, and Kevin tries to remember if they were ever that close when they knew each other. She'd always sort of intimidated him. Dancing impulsively toward strangers, singing songs in public. None of which was unusual among them, but with her it seemed genuine, not a show she was putting on to impress.

André rubs Kevin's stomach while he takes his order. André still looks the same, too. The same ponytail. The same fashionably gaunt look, which André always makes a point of attributing to diabetes, although the way he flaunted his syringes made Kevin a little suspicious.

"What's up with him?"

Susan exhales. "Who knows?"

André's been propositioning Kevin since the first time they met, but only in front of Susan, never alone. Sometimes he'd pick Susan up at Coffee People at the end of the night shift; as the three of them walked to the parking lot, André had once taken on the persona of a child molester. "Hey, little boy," he'd said, grabbing his crotch. "Want some candy?"

"Not tonight," Kevin had answered. "Besides, I've never been very good with my mouth." This was true; although he'd never tried it with a man, he'd always been enthusiastic with women, but his performance had suffered after a friend hit him a little too hard across the face and knocked his jaw loose. Now even a good kiss hurts him, reminds him of what happened, and Kevin wonders if kissing is what his friend really had in mind when he hit him.

Kevin orders the jambalaya, because he thinks he'd rather be in New Orleans, although he's never been there, only read about it.

André runs a hand through Kevin's hair. He's playing up the gay act, because at the next table there is a large group of Asian students, all coupled in a massive group date. André's more interested in getting a reaction from them than from Kevin, who's busy imagining they are a subgroup of some sort of Moonie wedding. He wishes things could be done that easily.

There's too much food to eat, and Kevin is distracted by Susan's questions about New York and her plans for a road trip to visit him there.

"I'll pick you up and we can drive to New Orleans," she says. And then Kevin notices a woman at the very next table, a woman with whom he'd had some involvement. A doctor's wife who used to send him prescription drugs through the mail when he couldn't afford to get them on his own. He feels like he should say hello to her but waits for her to make the first move. She doesn't, and he wonders if she hasn't seen him or, more likely, is pretending they have never met.

André brings out their leftovers wrapped in foil. He's sculpted Susan's into a fancy foil basket with a handle. Kevin's is in the shape of a giant erect penis that André rests on the table in front of Kevin's face. Kevin can feel the heat of the jambalaya radiating from the aluminum balls.

As they head out the door, Kevin looks across the room at all of the people seated. He's trying to decide which are locals and how many of them are like him, just passing through.

André drives them home, with Kevin seated alone in the back. They pass through the east side of the city, pockets of identical boxy homes, warehouses, a scattering of bars and nightclubs. André says, "Charity came back for a visit, did Susan tell you?"

"Yeah," Kevin says. "That's what she says."

There is a group of friends waiting in the living room. It's hard for Kevin to tell if any of them live there or if they just feel free to stop by anytime. They've got a couple of six-packs and a joint in circulation around the room.

Susan goes up to bed. Kevin wants to follow her but thinks it might be rude to André. He should stay and hang out, at least for a little bit. But as he sits listening to the conversation, he realizes he's made a mistake, because once he's decided to stay, he must stay for a certain period of time so it doesn't look like he's leaving out of boredom. He assumes the group in the living room are friends, but who knows, maybe they just met each other tonight. It's hard to tell from the awkward conversation, the long pauses; they may have just met, or maybe they know each other so well that conversation seems redundant. And he feels foolish sitting there witnessing it, thinking that in some way this is what he wanted so much when he was here: to have a group like this, to sit on the edge of the rug in a living room full of people. To have a home. But now it seems empty and unpromising. He can't help thinking of the customer-comment cards burning a hole in his pocket, waiting for his dissatisfaction. Then it occurs to him that even in his current state of passing through, a temporary visitor, he's more *here* than when he lived down the street. He wonders if his absence, his swing from left coast to right, can even qualify as an absence. He wonders about his apartment in New York and whether anyone notices he is gone. He goes to the phone to check his messages. There aren't any.

When Kevin returns, the talk has turned to Jason and the girl Jason had sex with the night before, on this carpet, in this room, with André in the corner the whole time watching.

"It was hot," André says.

"And you didn't want to join them?" someone asks.

"After a certain point I thought it would be wrong to interrupt."

Kevin watches as the conversation passes, as the small crowd responds to the story as they would a good commercial, momentarily captivating and instantly forgotten, and he wonders what is wrong with all of them, including himself. It's like there's a switch that's been turned off inside and they don't know how to turn it back on. How even the most intimate things exist only as anecdote. He wants to remember this, so he can tell his friends back in New York.

André disappears for a few moments, leaving Kevin alone in a roomful of strangers. He decides this is the perfect time to go to bed. He runs into André on the stairs.

"You're going to bed already?"

Kevin nods.

"You're going to sleep with Susan?"

"Well, I thought I would."

"Oh." André seems disappointed, but Kevin can't even begin to guess whom the disappointment is directed toward.

Even in the darkness he can make out the modeling shots that decorate Susan's walls. She tells him, still half sleeping, that she has to be at work at eight and she'll try not to wake him. He undresses quietly and carefully slides into bed next to her. He looks at the photographs on the the wall. You wouldn't know it was her if you hadn't been told. So thin, posing in cheesy glamour shots in pool halls, like a commercial for bad beer. In another, she's dripping wet, her hair cascading neatly down her face, her eyes closed in ecstasy. If she was awake, he'd ask her to tell one of her stories about modeling in Japan.

It is a deep sleep, the kind he gets only when he is traveling. It's like the vacuum of air travel, where nothing seems to happen, time doesn't even pass, as long as you are in the air.

In the morning Kevin cuts open the aluminum cock and eats the leftover jambalaya for breakfast. André comes downstairs, asking how he slept and surprised to see him packing so soon. André's wearing a T-shirt and nothing else, his own cock and balls hanging out for Kevin to see; André brews coffee and walks around the kitchen. Kevin wonders if he should take this personally, as some sort of invitation. He wishes he could drum up the interest. It feels almost like an obligation to take advantage of the suggestion, if that's what it is, but looking at André's spindly legs, he realizes it would be impossible. Besides, Kevin's never been convinced that the syringes André flaunts are really just insulin, and so who knows what he might catch.

Upstairs, Kevin finds a note from Susan on the opposite side of the futon. "Thanks for visiting," she says. "And remember, I'm coming to see you." The edge of the futon is damp, and he can see the remains of a puddle in the small space between the closet and where he slept. It is an almost perfect circle, half on the futon and half on the carpet, as if Susan had stood over him after she showered and before getting dressed. He presses his hand to the puddle and then raises it to his face. It doesn't smell of anything.

Kevin walks with his backpack over toward Hawthorne and then down toward the river, past the diners and coffee shops, past the Bagdad Theater, past the used-book and -record shops. There is a street fair happening, and everyone has set up booths on the sidewalk: vintage clothing and patchouli oil. Susan's right; this is where everyone has migrated. But they're all as indistinct as extras on a soundstage. Kevin looks up at the brick apartment house across the street. At the center of it, above the double doors that lead into the courtyard, a man is sitting in a large open window. He's got baggy shorts on, a beer in one hand, a good book in the other. The sound of a band warming up is drifting through the air. Kevin watches the guy for a few minutes. Watches his feet dangling over the edge. *A good view, a riff*. Kevin thinks, *He has everything I need.*

another shoot

There is no talk here of the industry, but you can imagine the establishing shot, panning over the desert, dollying across the motel parking lot and in through our window.

There is no dialogue, just the ambience of other guests walking past our door, unloading their cars, refilling their ice buckets, shouting requests back and forth from the open doors of their rooms somewhere above us. The sound of trucks passing over the wet pavement of the highway. The gentle hum of air from the vent. And the recorded horoscopes he makes me call over and over—even though they never seem to change—blaring from the speaker phone, only now there's a problem with the line, and instead of the recorded horoscopes, we hear the crossed lines of a hundred callers. Everyone speaks and no one listens.

He says, "Maybe we did something wrong." He says, "Maybe we shouldn't have called so often. Maybe they're mad at us." And then he lays his head down and everything is quiet, as if somebody has thrown an invisible sound blanket between us.

. . .

I might have asked if he approved of the decor. The orange carpet worn down from years of others like us passing through. The flake-board furnishings. The remote control clamped down so it can't be used. But I know by now that these are not the things he notices. What matters is the temporary shelter, the sense of anonymity. This is not the sort of place anyone would expect to find him.

It is not the sort of place I would expect to find myself.

Which is why lately I've taken to writing it all down, just in case things happen like we pretend they won't—just so if anything happens, you'll know I had nothing to do with it other than being here. This is what I've taken to doing lately, sitting with my pad and pen, wondering at him being twenty-three and already having more than he wants, nowhere to go.

When he first took me on, he warned me against it, warned me against writing anything down, told me about what happened to that kid in New York City, the one who worked with the billionaire, the billionaire who shot himself when he learned he had AIDS. This kid found himself out of work, unemployable because he knew the truth, had been witness to it and had written it down. Found himself out on the street for not pretending to know better. In fact, the kid was sloppy about it, kept his files right there in the office, under their noses, so what was he thinking?

Besides, he said when he hired me, "as long as you keep me relatively clean, we don't have anything to worry about."

Have to watch out for that word: relatively. What it relatively means is something fluid, whatever is to the advantage of the person speaking the word, as he speaks it. In this case it means keeping him clean enough that people will look the other way without feeling guilty.

I include myself when I say "people."

But I've taken to keeping a record, just in case it happens like we pretend it won't. I think it's okay, though. He doesn't know that's what I'm doing. That's what he pays me for anyway. Watching. He gets paid to be watched, then pays me to watch him. Except that what I watch is the truth. Not what all those pay to see on the screen. Watching him is like watching the tide go out and wondering if it will come back in. Once it does, I tear up the pages into pieces and leave them behind. Or, if I'm worried too much, I'll flush 'em.

I never use the needle on him myself. That's part of the deal. I don't want that. I'll help him find it, put it together and stuff, but if he can't find what it takes to shoot himself, then it's time to stop. That's what I figure. I'll help him find the vein, but I won't push the plunger in. I just take care of finding the place to stay, keeping track of the money, making excuses when his handlers call looking. ("Handlers," he says. "I don't have handlers. I just know a lot of really bored people with nothing better to do for five dollars an hour.") And lately I've been the one scoring it for him, 'cause I can tell he just can't think straight enough to make a deal for himself. You walk into those deals with those people, and they don't care who you are. They take what they can. He doesn't need any more of that than he's got.

Sometimes I catch him watching me. Him watching me watching him and so on. It's the game we play. Seeing how long we can go before one of us catches on that we're watching and cracks. He usually wins. He can go for hours just staring at me, not moving, not thinking a sound. I can't take that for long. That's why I've got my pad and pen. Lately he hasn't been playing that game, though. He's got a new one. It's like he's pretending not to be here at all. Like he's somewhere else entirely, left his body behind to keep a watch on me.

And when he does things, you'd swear it's the truth.

We might walk out across the painted desert, if I thought he was able. Out across the landscape that looks so flat and distant, he'd think it was a blue-screen projection in the state he's in. He doesn't even know he's due back tomorrow to start another shoot. It used to be that he'd clean himself up for work. Now he passes it off as character. Dirty realism. The people he works for, they don't care. They watch the truth the way most people watch movies, out of curiosity, to see how it'll turn out. Once it's over, they'll decide what they'd change, how to make it better, easier to be believed. The last shoot, they didn't care much as long as he showed up, stood on the mark, and got the words out. They dubbed the wild lines in later. Got great reviews. That's the one that put him over the top. The producers had been concerned, watching the dailies, watching the rushes, seeing how it seemed he needed to be held up, his scarecrow appearance, the loss of continuity. "Oh, no," the director said. "We're just experimenting. Improv, you know. Seeing how far we can take the character."

Now he can look any way he wants. They've even given him face approval.

. . .

When it comes to this hour of the night and I'm just sitting here—sitting here watching him flicker—that's when I think about what I'll do when he goes. What that billionaire's family did was have a plan. Do you think they wasted a moment mourning? No. They had other things to worry about. Kicked right into action once he did himself in. Got the family doctor to write something nice on the certificate. Got only the trusted staff to clear out all his toys, so by morning there was nothing left of his true life. So there'd be no questions. Well, there'd be questions but no proof. No proof of who he was. They call that family pride.

Proof. That's what I keep thinking. I mean, if it does happen one day, who's to say I knew any better. Who's to say I was here. Maybe I was in the other room, out in the car, nodded off. Who's to say I was here when it happened. Who's to say I could have made a difference. I mean, what if he was on his own this whole time, alone, who's to say things would have turned out differently.

So I'm just watching him slip out from under himself, a sense of calm that overtakes us, with just the sound of the passing trucks outside, the air circulating through the vent as ever. I run my hands along the frozen remote. I lift the receiver to call—too late—for help, or just to tell someone my job is over. But there is no dial tone, just a chorus of a thousand tiny voices, a universal party line, and all of them calling out as if someone might listen.

In their film version I'll act as consultant. We'll shoot this sequence in negative sound. Dub the wild lines in later.

This is the story of a man I have no interest in.

Stephen calls in the middle of the night—the middle of the night being, for me, twelve-thirty—he asks if I'd like to meet him for a drink. He does this occasionally, although it should seem strange that a kid I sort of work with, a kid ten years younger, just out of school, is calling me. But he does this occasionally, and I always answer. At first I would pick up the phone thinking that perhaps it was my husband, Sam, calling to tell me he'd been up late, too, thinking things through, wondering if he made a mistake in leaving me.

Of course, Sam would never do this, even if it was what he was feeling, so it was silly of me to indulge in this delusion, but otherwise, I might never have picked up the phone and wouldn't have spoken to Stephen. The last time Stephen called, I realized I was actually glad to hear from him.

"I just haven't heard from you in a while," he says. It was

true, I'd been avoiding him, sneaking by him on my way in and out of work, pretending I hadn't seen him.

"Okay," I said. I hadn't turned the lights out, in spite of the late hour. "I'll meet you."

It was Christmas Eve the first time Stephen hugged me, in the back storeroom of the bookstore, during the height of the Christmas rush. I was just getting off my shift—swing—and had gone back to dig my coat out of the pile near the coatrack; during the holidays there were too many temps for all of us to be guaranteed a spot, so coats were frequently left in mounds on the floor and on the folding chairs in the back. I was checking my pockets to see if anything had been stolen, but I couldn't remember if I'd left anything valuable in them, so I was standing looking a little lost when he walked up to me, gave me a halfhearted embrace, and wished me a Merry Christmas before continuing to the back to check on stock. The hug seemed less than sincere, more like the fulfillment of a dare, though it was hard to tell who the dare might have come from: himself or someone else. And I was hardly one to judge the sincerity of a hug, as Sam might say if he was speaking to me.

Stephen was just out of film school, but he held a supervisory position. He was in charge of blank books, bookmarks, audiotapes—everything in the store that didn't require actual reading. I, on the other hand, worked in the café.

Because we didn't work together, we'd never really talked before, though sometimes I'd notice him lingering at the juice refrigerator, acting as if he was having trouble making up his mind, and once, after closing, he'd asked if he could have a free drink.

"I can give you leftover coffee," I said.

"I was thinking of something else," he said, without naming it.

"Sorry, all I can give you is coffee."

So it was a surprise that he would hug me on Christmas Eve. And it made me nervous, because I'm the kind of person who should be kept away from romance, the way certain people should be kept away from guns or sharp knives. This is what Sam once told me (just after the divorce became final, when we thought we might remain jovial adversaries, meddling in each other's lives indefinitely), but when Sam said these words, he said *you* instead of *I*. "You are the kind of person who should be kept away from romance . . ."

Ours was an early marriage, done in haste after college, as if marriage would provide the final credits that were necessary to graduate and get on with our lives. We had that checklist mentality: things to do on the way to becoming like our parents. Once we completed marriage, we moved on to fancy vacations, a modest summer home, etc. And once his career took off, he encouraged me to quit my own, to stay home, to work in a small studio he rented for me on the top floor of a brownstone on the Upper West Side, to pursue my art. It was years before I realized that he wasn't encouraging my creativity but liked the idea of a woman who stayed home, the burden of supporting me giving him something to talk about over drinks after work. And it was in this way that I considered it that "he left me."

I initiated the divorce, which my lawyer advised me against, suggesting that if I could manipulate Sam into making the first move, I would be in a position to ask for more money. Fortunately, Sam's lawyer assumed I knew of his affair and offered a nice package deal in lieu of alimony. At the time, I was looking for simplicity and thought that I made out rather nicely: the studio, now converted to an apartment, and a dwindling lump sum of money.

At night sometimes I lie sleepless in the dark, the sound of water dripping, ticking, marking time as it passes. Like water torture.

The problem became what to do on weekends. I began to experience, for the first time since college, that sense that on weekends I was the only person who wasn't, at that precise moment, about to get laid. In the past I had relied on weekends for the quality of their emptiness. But with everything else so desperately empty, by the time the weekends came, I was out of my old tricks. Even window-shopping was out of the question. The shopkeepers had become accustomed to my presence. I appeared throughout the week like clockwork, doing the circuit, running from one store to another and lingering over objects I would never buy. Lace curtains, hand-forged cutlery, ceramics spun on a wheel, the latest season's clothes followed by the remainders. The shopkeepers eyed me suspiciously, as if I might be stealing. And maybe I was.

I spent Mondays reading the week's magazines without paying for them. A huge superstore had opened just down the street, and they allowed this kind of thing, perhaps thinking that if they lured me in with the freedom to browse, I might actually spend some of my nonexistent money there. What fascinated me about the place was the cavernous space of it, how it created the feeling of actually being somewhere, yet, when you took the time to look on the shelves, there was nothing really there. The stock made no sense to me. Stacks and stacks of books I'd never heard of, up and down the aisles there were some of the most illogical titles, but the things you would expect to find——Woolf for instance——were hard to come by. They'd placed large signs throughout the store. BECOME A BESTSELLER, they read. I decided to apply. In the space where they asked when I would be available to work, I wrote "weekends only," as if I had something more important to do during the week.

They offered me the choice of two positions: Café or Art.

"You're too smart to work with current literature," they said.

And so I spent weekends helping men older than myself select a book of Kate Moss photographs. I was new, so I didn't question the logic of classifying as art a book of cast-off fashion shots of a wafer-thin teenage model. When these customers asked my assistance, they showed no signs of embarrassment, in spite of the fact that the Kate Moss book, titled *Kate*, was amply displayed. Once I pointed it out to them, they looked at me helplessly, as if they required my assistance in turning the pages. It was then I decided the café might not be so bad and was granted a transfer.

I was the only person in the café without a personal beeper, without a string of personal phone calls pulling me away from the work. I stood with a pitcher of milk, steaming and frothing, looking out across the store at the couples strolling hand in hand, at the nannies with their charges heading into the children's section, at the teenagers looking for an easy pickup, at the stock boys carting away stacks of books to be remaindered or pulped.

I've become the kind of person who lies about her age.

It isn't really that I've reached the point yet where lying is a necessity. I'm no longer in my twenties but not yet nearing my forties. I'm at the point now where things might go one way or another. It is a comfortable stage to be at, but the comfort of plateau makes me uneasy. In certain circumstances, it is possible for me to fool myself into thinking no one notices. Working in the café, for example, it was possible for me to feel I was a peer of the kids working with me. As long as I was quick and put a skeptical curve on any observation I made, it was possible for me to believe they didn't notice that I didn't belong.

But as I walk through the bar—alone—on my way to meet Stephen, I imagine people are eyeing me, not as a conquest, but as a curiosity, as if I've come to pick up my son.

It was well into the New Year before Stephen and I had our first conversation, during the consumer lull that follows the holidays, after the last of the unwanted gifts had been returned or exchanged. By this time I knew that Stephen was a sort of pathological philanderer who had a particular fondness for seducing the girls in the art section. This made me feel safe for several reasons: It gave me a context, and, as I was neither a girl nor working in art, it was safe to assume I was out of the running.

One evening in the break room, I paged through Kate Moss's introduction to her book. In it, she voices her concerns over the burden of introducing a retrospective of her work at such a young age. I found myself feeling a certain amount of sympathy for her, for the fact that she considered standing before a photographer a demanding art, for the fact that she didn't seem to realize a day would come when no one would want to take her picture and she would be on her own.

Across from me, Stephen sat eating his dinner from a small plastic lunch box. On the side of the lunch box were terrible drawings of the Mighty Morphin Power Rangers. Stephen was, in fact, in his early twenties. The lunch box distracted me for two reasons. One, because it was made of plastic rather than metal, and I wondered at the fact that now everything seemed to be made from plastic. Disposable. Two, I remembered that when I was young, lunch boxes were passé by the second grade. We all insisted on bag lunches, to prove our maturity and independence. Lately, though, I'd been noticing an alarming number of adults carrying lunch boxes, some women even using them in place of purses.

Stephen looked up from his sandwich and asked, "How is that book? I've been meaning to read it."

"Heartbreaking," I told him.

"It's my birthday," he said.

"How old?"

"Twenty-two. How old are you?"

"Older than you think."

"We're going out afterward, to celebrate." He seemed to be waiting for me to invite myself along. Then he gave up on waiting and said, "You should come. Unless you have someone to go home to."

I smiled.

"That sounded wrong," he said. "I meant if you want to."

Then I said something that made me sound more interesting than I was. "Would it be okay to come if I have someone I don't want to go home to?"

In my studio there is a leaky skylight, something that provokes me, something that easily might be fixed, but I'm reluctant. Because I think of it only when it is leaking, and it leaks only when it rains, which is not a convenient time to do repairs. Then, when the weather clears up, I'd rather not think of the leak, so I allow myself to forget about it until the next storm. I could easily call the super, report the problem, and allow him to take care of it for me. But lately I've become reluctant to ask for anything. I tell myself I want to take care of things myself, refuse what help may be available to me, and then fail to make good on my promise to take care of things. I'd rather let the problems linger, keep me company, than get rid of them, or worse, discover in my efforts that I am incompetent.

The truth is, I guess, that none of it has anything to do with the rain. I've become the kind of person who fills her time with needless chores—like arranging my bookshelves by author one day, subject the next—in place of the things that really need my attention.

I mentioned the leak to Stephen, as he sat across from me one night, with his lunch box.

"Want me to take a look?" he asked.

I have to admit there was a certain charm to this misunderstanding. I shook my head. "No," I said, "I'll take care of it," knowing that this was not the truth.

That night, Stephen and I settled into the back booth and waited for the others to arrive.

"So what's your story?" he asked. "What are you doing here?"

I wasn't sure if he meant what was I doing working, or what was I doing with him, but either way I was impressed that he recognized that none of us seemed to be here, doing anything, entirely of our own conscious volition. So I told him the details of the marriage (which might have answered the question either way), the condensed version, making it sound vaguely entertaining, like a short trip abroad.

When the others arrived, they piled their coats on the next booth and the conversation moved on to more traditional topics, like customers upset that we couldn't identify the book with a blue cover that someone was talking about on TV (or was it the radio?) last month. The rest of the group left pretty quickly. Maybe it was because we were all worn out from work, or maybe it was the fact that Stephen and I kept talking to each other as if no one else was there.

When one of the managers asked why I seemed a little groggy the following day, I felt I had to explain everything. So I told her how, after the bar shut down, Stephen and I went back to his apartment and sat up all night watching old television on tape: *The Brady Bunch, The Mary Tyler Moore Show,* Bob Newhart when his wife was still Suzanne Pleshette. Things that had existed only in reruns for generations.

"Why didn't you go home? You don't live that far away," she said. "Why did you stay?" Her voice rose an octave as she spoke, as if I'd revealed an alarming character flaw, as if watching old television was the most intimate thing two people could do. As if we had shared something hidden.

Beers with Stephen became a regular, occasional thing after that. Usually just a drink or two and him asking about my life, how I was doing. Fine, fine. I usually didn't tell him the truth. We'd try to get the others to join us, but they would just nod their heads and say, "Oh, no, you two go ahead."

And nearly every night, when it was time to go home, Stephen would hug me on the corner before saying good-bye.

"You know you need at least eight hugs a day," he told me.

"Great," I said. "I just need to find seven more between here and my apartment."

Sometimes, around his friends, Stephen pretended he knew me less than he really did, which made me nervous, because when people act as if they know you less than they do, it almost always means they'd like to know you more.

Sometimes, while I was supposed to be serving customers, I would watch Stephen and his friends from the corner of my eye. I'd watch them out on the main floor, flirting with the teenagers who came in. On nights when I wasn't invited out with him, I wondered where he went, what he was doing.

Just out of curiosity. I didn't feel slighted. I had no expectations.

I imagined Stephen and his friends getting smashed and wandering back to his place to pop in a porno.

Sometimes I wondered what would happen if I were to bring Stephen home, but this fantasy faded when I imagined there would be instruction involved, not from lack of experience, but from lack of the specific kind of experience I needed, and how,

I wondered, could he give it to me, if he had never really experienced it himself?

I've become the kind of person who takes possession of things I have no use for.

There was a security guard who worked at the entrance to the store. I didn't know his name, but he was short and solid, a young man. He wore his hair cut short, nearly shaved, yet there was enough of it that I could not see his scalp. He was Hispanic, I believe, which I lately find I admire, and he had a nice smile, which he used with me too often. He smiled as I came in to work. He smiled as I left. There was a sincerity to it that disarmed me, made me feel as if he knew me better than he did. It made me wonder if he smiled at everyone that way. It made me think he knew I'd been stealing books and slipping them into my alphabetized shelves at home. Books I had no intention of ever reading. Even the *Kate Moss*.

More and more I found myself spending a night out with the guys after work. I found myself thinking of them as ''the kids,'' though I made a great effort—successful—never to say it out loud. Stephen would see me restocking the paper cups and shout, ''Don't go anywhere,'' because he knew unless he told me otherwise, I would.

The others in the café would tease me, they'd want to know the details of my nights out. If they'd seen me on the street, they wouldn't have given me any notice, but here, all of us working jobs we'd rather not have, lives bleed through onto each other like paint on raw canvas.

Tonight we sit at a back table in a bar down the street. The jukebox plays Springsteen, Sinatra, Billy Joel. "My Way" and "Uptown Girl." I feel caught in a time warp, a throwback to my college days. I do the math and discover what grade Stephen was in when I was in college. I undo the math and take a sip of my beer. Stephen indiscreetly points out a girl staring at us from across the room. He says, "Last week I kissed her."

"You don't sound too happy with that."

"It was probably a mistake. But you weren't here to stop me." Then he adds, "But she's a good kisser."

When she leaves, I wonder which of us is more relieved.

Then Stephen tells me what he was doing earlier, before he made the call. He says he visited his old girlfriend. He says, "I think we're getting back together."

I think, if they're getting back together, he should be with her now. *Why call me?* And I tell myself that this analysis is based on simple logic, devoid of any unexplored emotional attachments.

In the silence that follows, Stephen begins to tell me a joke.

I know immediately that I'll remember the punch line, because it is a joke in which the punch line is the entire point of the story. The bits and pieces that lead up to it are arbitrary— just an extended excuse to say, "I left my harp in Sam Clam's Disco." You could add it to the end of any story and get a smile. The point is just to get to the punch line, the bottom line. And it occurs to me that all these little meetings and late-night phone calls have been serving a similar purpose: meaningless in themselves and heading to some irrelevant conclusion. An ending that will have nothing to do with what came before or after it.

"You are the kind of person who should be kept away from romance . . ."

I thought at the time that he meant I was dangerous to others, but I've come to realize that what he meant was I am dangerous to myself. Of course, we're no longer speaking, so what he meant is a matter of interpretation, and my interpretation of people's motives has been known to be flawed, hence his comment, no matter what his intention.

Stephen tells me, "It's late. It might be dangerous for you to go home alone."

"You're right," I tell him. "I'll see you tomorrow."

. . .

I've become the kind of person who tells lies, who lies to herself, casually wondering how many steps exist between this and losing myself completely. Stephen sits across from me from time to time. He sits there, having no idea what it is he is witnessing: watching the final pieces of who I used to be waiting to be stacked up and remaindered.

a story about someone else

Mary sleeps in again. She can't tell if it's jet lag or being back in New York, or maybe she's having some kind of breakdown. She listens for Shannon——the sound of her going through the morning rituals, darting into the living room and around the hideaway bed Mary is sleeping on——and once it is silent again, Mary pulls the covers up over her head. She'll go out later. This afternoon. Tomorrow. She should call people and let them know she's in town, but now that she's actually here, she's worried that they might not care, or worse, they might only act as if they care when really they think her reappearance is an intrusion.

On the plane in from California, the woman sitting next to her was reading one of last month's issues of the *Bay Guardian*. Mary has every inch of that cover memorized, even though she hasn't bothered to look inside. It's the issue they printed her essay "Bad Habits" in, but she's afraid to look at it now, because she can't remember how much of what she wrote is true and how much of it was just her being clever.

I never realize that a relationship is what I've had until it's over. I always think of it in other terms. A friendship. Acquaintance. Affili-

ation. Infatuation. Association. Interaction. Intersection. Anything but a relationship. It isn't until I've lost it that I realize what it was was a relationship.

That's how "Bad Habits" began, on a scrap of paper, between interviews for two jobs she didn't get. Mary just started writing it, scribbling words on a scrap of paper, the way John used to doodle on cocktail napkins when they were together. It began as an accident and grew larger, until it was too big to ignore. In this way, she thought, the writing itself reminded her of the relationships she was writing about. Then, before she knew it, a friend of a friend offered to show it to someone, and the next thing she knew she was being introduced as the woman who had "a piece" in the *Guardian*. "A piece" that made people angry, because what "Bad Habits" was really about was her relationship with John. About how they did and didn't treat each other. About how, in the end, they were staying together only because they thought she might be pregnant. And how, in the end, she felt relief that it was over. What she was thinking but not saying, that's what "Bad Habits" was about.

Mary could tell the piece bothered people in New York by the way they grew silent when the subject came up, or how they wouldn't return her calls after she'd sent them a copy to read. Mary thought she knew what was bothering them. They were worried that she was talking about something painful instead of doing the healthy thing and pretending none of it mattered. Or maybe they were annoyed that she thought her life was important enough to write about.

And they might have been concerned about the fact that she used John's name.

In California, everyone seemed to think her writing about it was a great idea. At parties, people would introduce her as the woman who wrote "that piece" and then embarrass her by pulling out a yellowed copy from the recycling to show people who didn't remember having seen it. People were always agreeing that it was really "terrific." They wanted to share their own experiences with her, or even relive them. She thinks maybe that's the reason she never wants to go back.

The first thing Shannon said when she picked Mary up at La Guardia was, "You look great! Did you get a nose job?"

It was such a strange question, it took a moment to answer. "I have a perfectly fine nose," Mary said, covering it for a moment with her hand. "Why would I need a nose job?"

While waiting at the luggage claim—sure that her luggage would turn up missing—Mary went over in her head the list of things she would not discuss with her friends in New York. She would not reveal that her recent weight loss was caused by the fact that she can no longer afford to eat out and, rather than going to movies, which she also can't afford, she goes to the gym to work out on a friend's membership. She won't tell Shannon that. And Mary won't tell her that when she spent a hundred bucks at an outlet store, sprucing up her wardrobe for the trip, the American Express lady called her to the phone and told her that this would be absolutely the last time they would be able to approve a charge on the account.

"But I sent you a payment a few weeks ago," Mary had said.

"But you still owe us money," the AmEx lady replied.

At dinner her first night back, Mary ordered steak and watched as it bled across the plate when she stabbed it. Shannon ate a salad, making a big deal of her disgust at Mary.

"You know, when they hook electrodes to lettuce, they can register its screams," Mary told her.

"I saw John the other day," Shannon said. "He's really upset with you."

Mary said, "He usually is," even though she hasn't spoken to him since she left him last year.

"He's really upset about that piece you wrote. 'Bad Habits.' "

Mary put her fork down. "He read that?"

"Apparently."

"There's nothing in that piece he didn't already know about," Mary said, even though she knew that wasn't really true. What she meant was, there wasn't anything in it that she should have had to tell him.

"You said he was one of your bad habits."

"Well, it's not my fault if he recognized something." Suddenly Mary didn't feel very hungry. It hadn't occurred to her that he would care, but then she realized that she was concerned not so much with what this said about him—that he might still have feelings—as with what it said about her—that she might not have any.

"You used his name."

"He's not the only John I ever had," Mary said, looking up to see if Shannon would catch the pun and trying not to pay attention to the fact that she was suddenly feeling very stupid.

"I guess you should be proud. You really struck a nerve. You know John, he never shows emotion about anything, but he's been acting psychotic since he read that piece."

"Thanks," Mary said. "I feel much better." Actually, what she was feeling was that she shouldn't have come back. That she should call Nancy. Find an out clause. Nancy taught her always to find an out clause. Nancy has a stack of airline vouchers as an out clause. That's how Mary got back to New York, on one of Nancy's tickets. Mary likes to tell people that Nancy has at least one voucher for each of her failed relationships. She gets to the airport for that first extended vacation with the guy, but she always backs out. She used to tell the ticket agents: a family emergency. But now she's honest. "It's a mistake," she tells them. The ticket agents understand. They've been there.

"What was he doing reading the *Bay Guardian* anyway?" Mary asked. "I don't even know any San Franciscans who read it," she said, but of course she wasn't telling the truth.

"Maybe someone faxed him a copy."

Mary pushed her plate away. "I feel like I killed him. I feel like I did something I can't undo."

Shannon said, "Let's order dessert!"

Mary turns up the air conditioner and pulls the phone under the covers with her. She calls Nancy in Providence.

"I met a man," Nancy says.

"You always meet a man," Mary says.

"But I like this one," Nancy says.

"And you always like them."

"He invited me out to his yacht for a few days, but I'll be able to pick up my messages from the boat, so let me know if you're coming. I'll probably be using you as an excuse to leave early anyway."

Great, Mary thinks. I'm her out clause and she is mine.

Mary gets up and looks out the window. For a moment she thinks she can see John marching down the street in his leather jacket, his shoulders hunched forward, propelling him toward some goal. It's like he's hunting a wild animal that's been set loose in the city. Then Mary remembers that everyone walks that way in the city, and the figure disappears. It might have been anyone, she thinks.

She climbs back into bed and pulls the covers over her head.

Earlier, she could hear Shannon talking on the phone in the next room. She was talking to her ex-boyfriend Kim. Mary remembers warning her not to go out with a man named Kim, but she wouldn't listen, so now Mary gets to remind her.

"Didn't you guys break up years ago?" Mary always says.

"Yeah," Shannon says, "but we never stopped seeing each other."

Mary imagines their lives as a sitcom that would last six weeks on Fox.

This morning she could hear Shannon's voice rising on the phone. "Kim . . . Kim! KIM!" It made her think maybe John wasn't so bad. Suddenly she can only remember all of the things she wasn't thinking about when she wrote "Bad Habits." Like the way he would do little things without asking. Like buy her lemonade on the street when she didn't even know that's what she wanted until he handed it to her.

When Shannon gets back from work, she stands over the bed and tells Mary, "If you're going to slash your wrists, do it right. I don't want a lot of blood to clean up. In the bathtub, with the water running."

Mary says, "It's just jet lag," and imagines the kind of mail Shannon's comment would get on the Fox sitcom version of their lives. She imagines the sweetened laugh track.

Mary calls Providence and gets the machine. "I'm so miserable," she says. "You should be glad I haven't come to see you."

Mary's standing beneath the Calder mobile. She looks up, waiting for it to fall. When she hears a voice saying, "What are you doing here?" she assumes it's a museum guard. But it's not a guard. It's Ginger, John's sister. Mary always thought Ginger would be okay if only she didn't act like someone named Ginger.

"You look shell-shocked," Ginger says. "Like somebody hit you." She oversmiles like John. To Mary, it has the look of someone who doesn't like children being forced to talk to a five-year-old.

"I've been hiding out since I got back. You found me." Mary waits for a response, but Ginger's just standing there, like she doesn't understand. "Look," Mary says. "I know John's mad at me."

"You're being sort of ridiculous," Ginger says. "Just forget about it."

"Well, could you tell him if you see him?" Tell him what? Mary wonders. That she is sorry? She suddenly imagines the scene played out on a train platform, in soft focus, black and white.

"Sure," Ginger says. "And by the way, I'm having a party tomorrow night. It's Christmas in July. Wear red if you're up to it."

At Ginger's party, Mary's the only person wearing black. She's rehearsing all of the things she's decided not to tell John. She won't tell him it's good to see him; it would sound too rehearsed. She won't ask if he's upset or what he's upset about. "What do you think?" he'll say, as if they've already spoken about it. She's sure that if she tells him anything at all about how she's feeling, he'll think she's trying to start an argument, so she decides that if he shows up, she'll just apologize and leave before he has the chance to make her feel worse than she already does.

Mary tried to get Shannon to come with her, but she's waiting for a call from Kim, so Mary stands alone in a corner of the living room, watching Ginger run around in a little Santa suit, popping cherries soaked with vodka into the mouths of all the men. Mary notices how little the place has changed since the first time she was here, years ago, maybe even before John and she were a couple. It was just a bunch of singles then, and everyone was talking about the fucked-up couples they knew.

"You all sound so surprised," she had said. "Isn't every couple you know fucked in some way? Isn't it a requirement around here?"

John had looked at her and said, "We don't have a fucked-up relationship." Then he smiled, and she realized he was right. "Mary and I are lovers," he announced as a joke, but nobody laughed. Later that night, they went home together, and suddenly it was true.

Sometimes Mary wonders if the only healthy relationships are the ones that haven't actually happened yet.

At one A.M. Mary realizes she's probably been wasting her time. John hasn't shown his face. He knows I'm here, she thinks, so he isn't coming. But one of his friends keeps smiling at her from across the room, like if he smiles enough, she'll have no choice but to walk over to him. Finally he crosses over to the wall Mary has claimed as her own. She keeps thinking his name is Simon, but she knows she is wrong. She remembers that he and John grew up together. The same neighborhood in Queens. He and John used to say, "I'm gonna cut you, man," instead of hello. It was their running joke. Simon's smiling at her, as if he's glad to see her, but Mary knows it's a trick. The last time she saw him was just before she left town. She'd accidentally mentioned to someone that Simon's dachshund was leaving little puddles all over his apartment, and it turned out the person she'd mentioned it to was his super. So Simon showed up as she was packing her car and said, "I can make your life miserable."

"No, you can't," Mary told him. "I'm leaving."

"You don't understand," he said. "You don't know what I can do."

Mary imagined Simon and his dachshund following her across the country to make her life miserable, as if she wasn't capable of doing that on her own.

Now Simon's smiling at her in Ginger's living room. Simon says, "You're fucked up. Now that I know the way you think about people, I'm sorry I was ever nice to you. You have a lot of nerve coming here." And he's still smiling at her when he's done speaking.

Mary thinks of saying, "When were you ever nice to me?" but that's exactly the point. Everyone is upset with her for finally saying what she was always thinking. Now she's thinking that when he says she has a lot of nerve coming here, he doesn't mean the party, he means New York. As if it's his. She wants to ask him: I'm confused, are you someone important? But instead she just stares at him until he goes away. She feels like they both belong on a playground somewhere.

She heads for the bathroom. She doesn't feel well. She wants to go home—to Shannon's home, that is—but she thinks if she leaves now, it will look like she's leaving because John isn't here, rather than just because she's bored. She imagines her exit as a topic of conversation, with all of the people who haven't spoken to her offering their insights into her personality. Mary sits down on the toilet to think things through. She does some of her best thinking in strange bathrooms. Nothing to distract her except reading the labels on the back of shampoo bottles and assessing the choice of toilet tissue. Ginger's tissue is a sort of pale mauve. Mary thinks she might be getting her period. She imagines this is the reason for her mood. It has nothing to do with John. She searches through the cabinet for a box of tampons. She reads the back of the box.

Ginger pounds on the door. "Who's in there? Is everything okay?"

When Mary opens the door, Ginger falls in slightly before catching on to the frame. "Oh, it's you," Ginger says. "I was worried. At my last party, somebody locked herself in and threatened suicide. I was having visions of red."

"I'm fine," Mary says. "I'm leaving."

Outside, the city is dead. No traffic. Things seem submerged, an underwater city. Mary spots a man across the street from her, smiling. It's John. She crosses to him, and he stands over her, smiling.

"Mary," he says. "How are you doing?"

"I'm fine," she says, and as she says it, she realizes it's a lie.

His face changes, grows narrow and pinched. She remembers this look later, because that's when he hits her. A direct, premeditated punch across the nose for maximum impact. So perfect a shot, witnesses would swear he'd been practicing, but nobody sees it. The street is empty.

And then he is gone.

Mary raises her hand to her face, thinking she's going to laugh, but instead she watches blood pour out into her hand and down her arm. She knows what to do with a nosebleed, she gets them often, so often, in fact, that John once accused her of having a secret coke habit. But she doesn't apply any pressure now to stop the bleeding. Instead leans her head forward, directs the blood away from her with one hand, and walks back to Shannon's.

If I'm bleeding, she thinks, it must be over.

In the lobby, she thinks how convenient it is to have the intercom speaker mounted in the wall, rather than a hand-held receiver. This way, she can call Shannon without bleeding all over it.

"He broke my nose," is all she can say. It's too difficult to say anything more with blood gushing over her lips. Shannon doesn't really understand until she comes down and sees the streaks of blood that have struck the wall beneath the intercom and the puddle at Mary's feet. Mary can see that Shannon is speaking to her, but she can't make out the words. Later she'll remember what she said was "He must have really been in love

with you to do something like this.'' Shannon doesn't say anything more until they get back to the apartment and Mary
reaches for a towel to wipe her face. Shannon says, ''Be careful!
It stains!'' And then Mary sees that Shannon catches herself,
and the life leaves her face for a moment, as if there is regret
floating somewhere beneath the surface, looking for a way to
escape.

At the hospital, one of the attendants hands Mary a rubber glove
filled with ice. Actually he tosses it to her, and it lands on the
floor near her feet. It takes her a moment to figure out what it's
for. She waits twenty minutes for someone to take down the
information. No one asks how it happened or if she's okay. They
want her name and billing address. In the space that asks for the
name of the responsible party, she begins to write ''John . . . ,''
but then she realizes they want to know who will pay the bill.
She waits for another half an hour before someone looks at her.
Shannon's in the waiting room, reading the current issue of
Cosmo.

A woman in a lab coat asks Mary if it hurts. The woman puts
on rubber gloves before she touches Mary's nose. Then Mary
remembers: the blood. The woman leads her to X-ray and another twenty minutes' waiting. She is led to a table, told to lie
down. Her nose is swollen and clogged with blood. It is difficult

to breath. Another twenty minutes. She stares at the reflection of her nose in the glass above her. It seems so clear now that this is what it comes down to: something small but significant. Something that will always be with her.

She is led to a chair in the corner of the hall. They tell her to wait. It seems there are no other patients, but she knows this isn't true. Still, she thinks, this is what I will tell people. That there were no other patients and I was made to wait hours. It is another twenty minutes. She watches an elderly couple as they come down the hall. They approach the desk, and the woman says, "He's having trouble breathing again." The woman has her arm around her husband's shoulder for support. She brushes his back softly with her hand. She tries not to show him she is worried. Mary thinks, they're in love the way my parents were. Till the end. The doctor sees them immediately.

Finally someone calls Mary to the desk. She thinks it's a doctor, but she's not sure. "There's no damage," he tells her. "Go home."

"How much is this going to cost me?" she asks.

"You'll have to talk to the receptionist."

She walks back to the reception desk, but there doesn't seem to be anyone there. This is what she will tell people. This is what it comes down to: another bill she can't afford to pay.

. . .

Mary stays in bed in the morning. Shannon's in the other room, talking on the phone with Kim. It sounds like they're getting back together.

Mary remembers the arguments she and John had in their final days. Anything she said was wrong. He'd show her some sketches—odd little things, like locomotives with cockroach legs—and she'd tell him how neat they were. "Yeah," he'd say, and pull them away, as if she wasn't to be believed. If she offered any criticism—like, "It's a locomotive with cockroach legs, what does it mean?"—he'd say, "Yeah," and pull the sketches away, as if he should have known she wouldn't understand. Eventually Mary stopped saying anything at all.

Once, he said, "I don't know why I bother sharing any of this with you."

And Mary said, "Neither do I."

She remembers they even had an argument about God. She never argues about God, rarely even thinks of Him. But one day toward the end, John made some comment about how silly it was that anyone still believed in God, and Mary said, "You don't really think that way."

"Don't I?" John asked.

"You have to believe in God," Mary said, not even looking up from whatever it was she was doing.

"Why?" John asked, sounding as if he was really expecting an answer.

"Well, maybe not God," she said. "But you have to believe in something."

"Why?" he asked. But this time it sounded more like a demand, and Mary looked up at him. It was then that she realized John was the kind of man who could never really believe in anything. She remembers now that he had that look then, the look he had last night just before he hit her.

Shannon hangs up the phone and sticks her head through the door.

"He was going to hit me anyway," Mary says. " 'Bad Habits' or not."

"Probably," Shannon says. "That's what men do." Then she just walks out of the room as if there's nothing more to say. Mary wants to be angry with her, but she doesn't have the energy for another fight.

Later, when Shannon returns for dinner, she asks Mary, "What did John say to you last night?"

"Nothing," Mary tells her. "He just hit me and left. Why?"

"I ran into him today," Shannon says. "I asked him why he looked so happy, and he said, 'Because I got the last word.' "

Mary sleeps in again. She knows it isn't jet lag anymore. She calls Nancy. She keeps thinking that if she were Nancy, she'd be able to get some kind of voucher out of this thing. She gets her machine and tells her that she's taking the next train to Providence. As she packs up her things and begins to make the bed, a bloody towel falls out onto the floor. It's the towel Shannon gave her to cover her face when she put her to bed that night. "New sheets," Shannon had said. Mary picks the bloody towel up and turns it in her hands. She remembers an exhibit John once took her to, a form of primitive art, designs on fabric using the artist's blood. The images were beautiful. She looks at her own blood dried on the towel. It doesn't seem so shocking anymore. It's only half bloody. If it had turned all red and dried in a crusty lump, she'd have had it wrapped and sent to John as a present. Christmas in July. As it is, it would be a disappointment. A shrug.

In the lobby Mary passes the super, still scrubbing the last of the blood from the walls. The streaks on the wall below the intercom are still faintly visible, but no one would guess what they are. A memorial to the two of them, and to bad habits.

Mary can see Ginger's head bobbing toward her in the crowd at the end of the block. Ginger looks as if she's treading water, her head disappearing beneath the surface and coming back up for a gulp of air. As they get closer, Mary sees Ginger is squinting at her, like she's staring into the sun. Mary thinks of all the things she'd like to do to her. Stick cherry bombs in her nose and light the stems. Ginger stops at the window of a shoe store and pretends to look in. Mary thinks, she's really just looking at her own reflection, checking to see if anything shows.

As Mary gets closer, she hears Ginger whisper, "Just keep going."

Just keep going. It could mean a hundred different things.

Once Mary's settled into her seat on the train, she begins to rehearse the story she'll tell when she arrives. By the time she gets to Providence, it will seem clever and witty. People will laugh when she tells it at parties, and no one will feel too bad for her, even if they notice that her nose is still too swollen for her to breathe. It will become a story that's repeated, by friends to acquaintances, by acquaintances to strangers. It will be discussed at offices and dinner parties, by people Mary has never even met. Soon it won't even be a story about Mary anymore.

It will become a story about someone else.

My apartment has two windows. One looks east, over the hedges in the park across the street and into the rose garden. The other window is in the back, where the building looks in on itself, down its hollow center, past the fire escapes lined with dead brown potted sunflowers, to the empty courtyard below. In the morning, I sleep until the sun rises in the east window and wakes me, then I look out over the park, across the green, into the garden spotted with bright red roses. There's a bunch of vine-covered trellises and arches leading in and out, and marble benches that seem left from a civilization that has passed. There's always someone waiting there, for an exchange of some kind.

If I stick my head out the window, I can see farther, past the reedy swamps of the park, to the edge of the victory gardens, with the gray skyscrapers looming above. I can see someone has torn the flyers down again—just four yellow corners remain stapled to each of the trees that line the street.

I know what the triangles mean. I've seen one of the flyers

intact. "Don't go in the park at night," it read. "Men have been raped and killed there."

The rumor was that they found a man's body in the rose garden, with a noose around his neck, but there was nothing in the papers. All those screams I heard in the night, I thought they were just someone's idea of fun. But I'm not worried. I don't pull dates often.

I don't pull dates often. I don't need the money. Sometimes I need the money. Sometimes I need the money, but that's not why I do it.

Jack was the first. He just followed me home one night. He wasn't the first to follow me home. At night the street is full of men looking. (Once, a guy even turned his car backward in the street—a one-way street—so he could face the traffic and eye the guys cruising by in their cars.) So Jack followed me home one night, and he was the first one I let in. I wasn't going to at first, but Jack had balls. He followed me right into the lobby. I had to slam the glass door in his face, but then I turned around to see who it was who had followed me so far. To see who had the balls. And there was Jack wearing that thin, tired expression that all family men have. He reached into his pocket and pulled out his wallet, waved his wallet at me from the other side of the glass. I caught a glimpse of his wedding ring and invited him in, because I knew it would be dangerous for both of us.

We didn't talk at all on the five flights up to my apartment. We just acted like we knew exactly what we were doing. Like it had all been planned out. Except that I have one of those tricky locks on my door: a metal rod that slips into a notch on the floor and a groove in the back of the door, so I can keep anyone out if I want to. Only the pole's a little too short and slips out sometimes and gets wedged somewhere it's not supposed to, so even I can't get in. So that's what happened when we got to my door. It wouldn't open, even for me.

"Wait here," I told him, and I went down a flight of stairs, through the window, climbed onto the fire escape, past the dry sunflower stalks and the rust-stained blanket hanging over the side, to my window, the whole time hoping the fire escape wouldn't break loose under my weight.

Jack stayed the night, which surprised me, but I guess I shouldn't have been surprised, considering how much he gave me. It wasn't until later I figured out an appropriate price scale for my time: an equation of how bored I'll be divided by how bored I am. So Jack stayed the night, and when I opened my eyes in the morning, I caught him pulling on my clothes.

"Those are mine," I told him. "Yours are over there."

I still don't know if Jack's really that absentminded, but one thing I've learned is that it's always the men who end up clinging most, in spite of themselves. Sure they try to bargain, but they're willing to pay more in the end. They act like it's all a simple transaction, but in the end they linger, sleep late, want to have breakfast in the morning. They pretend they're just too lazy to get up and leave, so I have to lie to them.

"I have another appointment," I tell them. "You'll have to leave."

So I ran an ad when I decided it was time to drum up business. Not that that's why I do it. Nothing fancy, the ad, just a few lines in the back of a local paper: my name (not my real name), my number (a voice-mail account), and a few of my most vital statistics. Lois was the first. Very businesslike, requested a meeting, discussed the terms. Women are easier. Thrifty, but they know a bargain when they see one.

"How does this work?" Lois asked.

"How do you want it to work?" I answered.

So we struck a deal. Something she liked to describe as "mutually beneficial." Mostly in private, occasionally dinner at a restaurant, where she'd get away with introducing me as her "young friend," because she was the kind of person who could get away with that. Lois had a father, several husbands, and grown sons, so she knew enough never to ask a man "Why?," so she never asked me, and I never asked her. That was our arrangement. It was mutually beneficial.

But Jack gets to be a little too much sometimes. Once, after I'd discovered that he wasn't really married—the ring was on the wrong finger (I always mix that up)—Jack told me, "You're too nice to be involved in something like this."

I said, "So are you."

There are others, lots of others. But most don't come back, even when they say they will, and they usually say they will. That doesn't bother me—that they don't come back—in fact, I appreciate it. It's safer that way. Less chance that they'll get confused about what it's really about. There's the couple from Cambridge with their kids in the next room, the boy from Arlington who must have saved all the money from mowing lawns in the summer. People in town on business are the best, likely to forget my number by the time they return. Sometimes I pretend I'm asleep when it's over, just lie there and wait for the floorboards to squeak as they sneak their way to the door.

Regulars can be trouble, because you can't rely on them. Like this guy last night—he went kind of nuts on me. I should have known he'd be trouble. I'd worked for him before. From the beginning he talked to me as if he thought I was actually listening. Too much eye contact that first night, I guess. So I finally decide it's time to cut him off, and he won't take no for an answer. Waits for me outside of my building. Makes a scene almost. Before dark even, so everyone could see. Starts demanding to see me. Follows me inside and up five flights, even though I won't even look at him.

I could run up to the roof, escape that way, tripping on the junkies huddled there in the door. They might follow me out onto the roof and invite me to join them. I'd smoked with them before, not wanting to disappoint them. We smoked the white paste from a Baggie they had, still soft, like it wasn't ready to be used, and it made my mouth numb, like drinking rubbing alcohol or getting novocaine. Then I looked out over the city, picking out houses where Jack and Lois might live, where they might be getting ready for bed, sitting in bathrobes in their kitchens, drinking hot milk.

But I didn't go to the roof last night, I went straight to my apartment and slammed the door on this guy. But he slammed it back on me before I had a chance to secure the lock, slide the rod into place. He slammed it back at me and sent the curved end of the rod straight for my head, right above the eyes. I could feel the sticky trickle of blood down my nose as I headed for the back window.

I crawled out across the fire escape, like crawling out across someone's ribs, flakes of rust embedding in my hands. I crawled between the dried brown stalks of sunflowers and pulled the stiff, rust-stained blanket over my head. He didn't see me. It was like I didn't exist anymore. Like I was nothing. Nothing left of me. He stuck his head through the window and stared right at me, but he didn't see anything at all. Just dead plants and dirt and rust waiting to be picked up by the wind.

I slept there and dreamed I was hanging. Hanging from the fire escapes, the fire escapes hanging from the building like metal skeletons, a dry stalk wrapped around my neck. This was my choice. Hang or fall. Fall down the center and disappear into the earth. I woke up before I could choose. The sun was shining down through the dry leaves, so dry I could almost see through them. My face was resting in the potted earth. And I could smell it on me, in the leaves and dust and dirt, in the cold clay pressing on my skin, in the blood on my face, blood dark and shriveled like a dry rose petal.

In the window across from me, a woman was standing in her bathrobe, a cup of coffee in her hand. She wasn't alarmed, just staring at me, concerned, knowing something was wrong, out of place. I climbed back into my apartment through the window.

Things are missing but I can't figure what. There are empty spaces that used to seem full. I can't decide what used to be there.

From my front window I can see someone has taken the flyers down again. People are gathering in the garden. Men, women, couples. Families with children. There's a red carpet laid down the center of the garden. A trellis arching over the head of a preacher dressed in black. A veiled woman in white is taken down the aisle. A man in a tuxedo is waiting for her. The scene is as flat and still as a painting.

From the distance, I imagine that the woman is Lois and the man is Jack.

It was on Magazine Street, in the lower Garden District, that I first met Pete. He was standing between the pillars of a dilapidated mansion where I had an appointment to look at an apartment for $150 a month—which I thought I could afford once my unemployment came through. The caretaker of the property was pudgy and old and couldn't stand up straight. He nodded toward me when I walked through the gate. "I had an appointment," I said. The caretaker nodded again at me and once more at Pete before he hobbled out the gate and down the street, never to be seen again.

"You don't want to live here," Pete said. "We can find something better."

I'd seen him before, hanging out at the hostel where I'd been staying. Pete had been staying there, too, before he had been asked to leave. That was the rumor, but you never knew what to believe. Something about money owed for his room. But he still kept coming back, looking for new friends. He'd been hanging out in the lobby that morning, listening to me make appointments for apartments all over town, including this one on Magazine Street.

"You stole my appointment," I said.

Pete said, "You were late." He lifted his backward cap and ran a hand through his black hair before replacing the cap. His hair, cut in a straight line, hung from beneath the edges.

"I was trying to make up some kind of résumé," I said. I'd spent the morning in the French Quarter, sitting at Kaldi's coffeehouse listening to jazz and trying to decide what kind of résumé to make. If I listed the good jobs I'd had over the years, I might seem overqualified for the kind of job I was likely to get. But if I cut them out, people might wonder what I'd been doing all this time. So mostly what I'd done that morning was look at my reflection on the side of the giant brass urns.

Pete said, "I'm trying to get through life without ever having a résumé." He said it as if it was meant to soothe me or to reassure himself that everything was okay, that everything would be taken care of. That's when I knew I wanted him as a friend, because I knew he couldn't be trusted. And as long as I couldn't trust him, he would never disappoint me.

Of course, my judgment was sometimes questionable. When my car broke down outside the youth hostel on Carondelet Street,

I mistook it for a sign that I had come to the right place, in spite of the fact that the hostel had burned down the year before and was now operating out of a much smaller house next door. The lace balconies I'd admired in the brochure stood intact, but the charred core of the house could be seen leaking out from small openings: from the edges of windows and the spaces between the door frames and the actual doors—small spaces you wouldn't notice if it wasn't for the dark soot and ash bleeding through the seams to warn you that something was wrong.

I'd planned to sell my car once I got there—to help cover expenses until I figured out what I was going to do—but in the first few days, the car slowly disappeared, first the hubcaps, then the antenna, the mirrors, until finally there was nothing left but a shell and I had to pay money to have it removed. Then I looked at the empty spot that remained and watched as other cars came to fill the space I had left behind.

After a few days, I noticed that everyone at the hostel had religious names. Everyone except me. Noah slept in the bunk opposite mine, and next to him was Joseph. There was a succession of Jasons, and in the bunk above mine, a man whose name nobody knew. In the middle of the night, his arm would hang over the edge of the bunk, pointing down at me like the hand of God. It was time to move.

. . .

Pete led me in through the front door of the mansion, which had been left unlocked. From the outside, the house held the illusion of being something that had once been great but had somehow lost its greatness. But from inside I thought perhaps it fell into another category altogether—greatness that had always been lost, that had existed only in potential.

A gray dust covered everything, as if the mansion was under construction. Cobwebs hung like cheesecloth in every corner and from what used to be a chandelier dangling from above. It smelled of urine, like people had been wandering in during the night to relieve themselves. Pete took me upstairs. He pointed to the padlocked doors and their frames. Their surfaces were covered with scars.

"People must break in all the time," he said. "You wouldn't want to live here. We can find something better."

He hadn't yet noticed the tiny scar beneath my left eye, a scar small enough that most people thought it was a birthmark. He hadn't run his finger over it, hadn't yet wondered if maybe, in some way, it was similar to the marks that covered the walls— left behind by someone trying to get inside.

Pete decided we should get something to eat. He said he knew a place where we could get free sandwiches and all we had to do was listen to this guy and his mother preach for a little bit. I said I thought I'd rather pay money, even though I didn't really have any. So Pete took me to the Please-U Restaurant on St. Charles instead.

"I like the name," I said.

I had moved to New Orleans at the end of January, because I couldn't think of anything better to do and I figured at least I'd be warm. I'd been staying in a friend's basement in Portland, sleeping on a mat on the floor of the room that had been her daughter's before her daughter ran away. She said I could stay with her as long as her daughter was on the run. I'd just been fired from my job—graveyard shift at Kinko's, making copies for schizophrenics from a halfway house nearby—and hadn't planned to stay long but hadn't planned on what else I might do, either. Mostly I sat in the living room waiting for the sun to come up, but that seemed to rarely happen. Sitting across the booth from Pete, I realized he probably wasn't much older than my friend's daughter; I wondered if he knew that I was nearly thirty.

The first few days in New Orleans, I mapped out the town through my sense of smell. The lawns of uptown mansions were marked by something sweet, with occasional drafts of smoke like burning leaves. Clouds of dust rose behind the streetcars on St. Charles. In the Quarter, on Decatur Street, the days were filled with the scent of powdered sugar rising from the beignets of Café du Monde, replaced at night with the acidic odor of the vomit and urine of drunken tourists; but somehow the sugary smell lingered and stayed with me, stronger than anything else.

Measures of time and money were mutable. It might be Tuesday or Thursday or Saturday. No one ever seemed to know for sure. Two minutes, two hours, two days, two months. A person's cash might last a week or be gone in an afternoon. I was searching for a little stability.

"Come on," Pete said, holding a corner of his muffaletta to my mouth. "You have to at least try it."

I shook my head. "I know I'm not going to like it," I said. Pete rolled his eyes at me, like he should have known. He told me about how, since he left the hostel, he'd been staying with this girl, but it wasn't very much fun. He said, "I mean, she invited me. I thought it would be . . . you know . . . fun." But the night before, she'd brought some other guy home and ended up fucking him in the living room. Pete said, "I mean, what the fuck is that?" He didn't want to go back there.

"I wish I had something I could do tonight," he said. "You know?"

"You want to go for a drink?" I asked.

Pete had even less money than I did, but he had a stockpile of food stamps. At the end of the meal, I gave the waitress a credit card I would never pay off that had a little bit of space left on it, and Pete paid me back in food stamps, giving me a little extra but not as much as I would have liked. Later, when I'd run out of money and was living on a ration of ramen noodles, I redeemed the food stamps one at a time at the Time Saver. Sometimes I would splurge on the two hot dogs for a dollar. On really bad days, I'd spend the extra quarter for cheese.

Pete had some stuff he was carrying, and he said he didn't want to be bothered keeping track of it if we were drinking. Mostly what he had was a little survival book about how to cook over an open fire and how to make lemonade out of ants. He'd been scribbling phone numbers on it all day. We stopped by the hostel, and I stuck it beneath my bunk and hoped no one with a Bible name would try to steal it.

It was raining in the Quarter, and everything was dead. Everyone who had been there the week before was gone, and the people coming to replace them hadn't arrived yet. We bought jumbo drinks from the Daiquiri Shoppe and wandered around looking for people having fun, but we couldn't find any. Even Bourbon Street was abandoned. The barkers outside the topless joints had no one but us to bark at, and what's the point of going inside if no one else is going to be there. Through the open doors, we could see kids in G-strings—girls in some, boys in others—dancing on bartops for just a few drunken patrons.

I showed Pete the place on Royal Street where I received mail. It was like a miniature post office, and during the day a woman sold stamps over the counter and gave good advice about things like where to eat and live. I hadn't gotten any mail yet—I was waiting for my unemployment claim to come through— and since I didn't have any money, most of the woman's advice was useless to me. I had a key to get inside after hours to check my box. I showed Pete my empty box, and we left again to head for Decatur, toward the smell of powdered sugar and alcohol and the more acidic odor of what they eventually became. As we left the lobby and shut the door behind us, Pete said, "I guess you could always sleep in there."

We rode the streetcar back uptown, and when I got off at the hostel, Pete took my hand and told me he'd be in touch, which I took to mean we'd never speak again.

I pulled Pete's survival guide from beneath my bunk. In the light from the window, I read about how to make soup from the bark of trees.

Noah was snoring in the bed opposite mine. A stranger's arm hung down from above me. A slip of paper fell out from the middle of the book. A court summons from Hawaii. Theft charges of some kind. The date of the trial had been moved so that Pete could return to L.A. and care for his ailing grandparents, but he'd come here instead.

I was worried about whether or not my unemployment claim would be approved, whether my cash would hold out long enough. I'd already begun running a tab at the hostel, even though I didn't know when the money might come through. Carnival was approaching, there weren't many apartments to choose from, and all the landlords in town knew they could make more money renting week to week to tourists until the season died down. I didn't expect to hear anything from Pete—

particularly now that I knew he was a criminal—so I started looking at apartments with other people.

First was another guy from the hostel, who slept with an AA bible under his arm. Sometimes, he said, he could find several meetings to go to in one night. He liked going to meetings, he said, because it was a great way to meet people, but he'd never bring home a girl he met at a meeting. "It's an illness," he said, "and why would I want to be with someone who's sick?"

"I'm really not sure about this," I said. It was fine if he always had to be thinking, but I didn't think it was necessary for me always to have to hear about it.

"What?" he asked.

"It's nothing personal," I said. "I just don't think I could live with someone who actually believes in something."

I met another guy on the streetcar. He had bad wired dreads, but there was a sadness about him that seemed nice. When I walked out to his house in the Marigny to meet him the following day, I found him still asleep in a corner of the living room and his roommates snorting crystal meth and trying to pack. "We only have a day to get out of here," one of them said as he wiped his nose.

Once I'd roused the guy with the dreads, we walked farther into the By-Water to see a half a double-shotgun that had been advertised for rent. The owners were having an open house, and we were the only people there who weren't a married couple. The place had been completely redone. Hardwood floors, fresh paint, glass cabinets built into the walls. All the surfaces were smooth. There were six rooms at least, one leading into the next. It seemed you could walk into it forever. While the guy with wired dreads was in the bathroom getting sick, one of the women explained that the family had owned the house for generations and wanted responsible renters.

We filled out an application anyway. On the way back to his house, he talked about how great it was going to be, how much fun we would have.

When I told him, "They're never going to let us live there," he started to cry.

Drinking coffee in Kaldi's, I'd found a discarded guide to Carnival that had fallen out from the center of the local paper. Parades during Carnival wind their way through the city, zigzagging through checkerboard neighborhoods several times a day, stopping traffic, though since it's Carnival, there isn't any traffic. It's everyone's last chance for fun before giving it up for Lent. They all go out to the parades, or, if they're lucky enough to be invited, they're in one, riding on floats lit with bare bulbs, their faces masked by hoods, tossing down doubloons and cups and beads all bearing the insignia of their krewe—Bacchus, Orpheus, Rex, Pegasus . . . The city hums with the electric generators of the parade floats. Women in the crowd flash their breasts to get the best beads thrown at them, the men on the floats being driven safely past them, the men on the floats masked, so they can ask for whatever they want and usually get it.

People come in families, fathers holding children on their shoulders to see, or in packs of male or female, crossing lines occasionally for an anonymous kiss. The grass medians where the crowds gather to fight for gifts from the krewemen are known as Neutral Ground.

On the night of the Bacchus parade, I stood on Neutral Ground on the corner of St. Charles and Napoleon, watching as plastic cups, beads, cards, and other treasures showered down from the passing floats and into the hands of the people in front of me. Watching how the New Orleans night air doesn't conduct light, how the light seems to collect in the air just around the bulbs, so only the richest krewes' floats look bright at all and even they are surrounded by an immediate darkness.

Henry was having a party on the other side of Napoleon. I'd met Henry house hunting, too, but we decided things wouldn't work out. His landlord was selling the house he was renting, so they were having a big party before they had to leave. He said I should come. I sort of hoped I'd run into Pete in the meantime, so I'd have someone I could take along, but I couldn't find him.

Maybe it would be easier to go home with someone if Pete wasn't around. That would be my goal. I'd walk into the party with being taken home as my only objective. It didn't seem to matter who took me.

A band called Lump was setting up to play in the main parlor, the beer was in the backyard. I leaned against the back of the house and watched a girl fumbling with the keg. There were two guys standing near her and some sort of slapstick comedy going on between them regarding the keg hose. She looked across the yard at me and smiled. She was cute in a New England sort of way. She looked wholesome but sexy, like a movie star playing a nun—she had that kind of face. She walked toward me with her beer, tripped over a bag of garbage in the middle of the yard, and managed to maintain her balance and her eye contact the entire time.

"I was wondering if you'd help me," she said. "My friends are having a contest, and I want you to help judge."

"What's the contest?"

"They're arguing over who has the biggest dick," she said. "Do you want to help me?"

"Can't they figure it out for themselves?" I asked. I looked over at the guys. They were still fiddling with the hose.

"That's exactly what I was thinking," she said. Her name was Amy, and she began admiring my beads. "You have a lot of them. Did people actually throw them to you?"

"Yeah," I said. "Sort of. I mean, I decided I'd never get

anything if I tried, so I just caught the things that everyone else missed.'' I had about a dozen strands of beads around my neck, and a stack of plastic cups for my new apartment, if I ever found one.

"Exactly,'' Amy said. She looked back at the two guys and the keg. "Look at all these,'' she said. Her neck was covered with big gold beads, countless strands of them. The kind that were saved for women who bared their breasts or gave blow jobs in the street. "I didn't want any of these. They just kept throwing them at me. Do you think it's sexist?'' she said.

"Do I think that if you're a woman you're more likely to get something?'' I asked. "Yes.''

"Do you want some of my beads?''

"Sure,'' I said.

She began pulling strands of beads over her head and lowering them over mine. The two guys came over and watched. Finally one of them said to her, "Do you want to fuck him? Is that what this is about?''

Amy just laughed at him, and he and his friend stepped away. "I think we're going to leave and go somewhere else,'' she said. "Do you want to go with us?''

"I don't know,'' I said. "I mean, am I going to be harassed?'' I just wanted to take her somewhere and hold her hand, but I couldn't think of anywhere to go.

She looked over at one of the guys and said to me, "He's not my boyfriend. We just always end up together.''

"Okay," I said. It seemed like it could be fun.

The four of us headed out and across Napoleon, wading through the debris of the parade: plastic cups, beads, playing cards, and toys that people had caught and then immediately discarded. Truckloads of prisoners were arriving to clean up after us. Amy and I were walking ahead of the guys. "Can you believe this stuff?" she said.

"The first parade I went to I thought it was ridiculous how people were fighting over these stupid toys," I said. "Then I suddenly found myself wrestling an old woman to the ground for a plastic doubloon."

Amy laughed. "Then, once you get your hands on the stuff, you wonder why you ever wanted it."

"Exactly," I said.

After the four of us had squeezed our way onto the crowded streetcar, the guy Amy usually ended up with began whispering to her. A drunken whisper, so I thought I could hear him saying, "I think your friend needs to get fucked." When Amy pretended not to understand, he added, "And I'm just the person to do it." She winced.

The streetcar engine whined and pulsated and made a rhythmic pumping sound that the tourists mistook for trouble. To me it always sounded like the ticking of a watch dropped into a box of kittens. It could lull you to sleep if you wanted it to.

I looked over at Amy and her friends and remembered that these kinds of things are never as much fun as they should be.

A penny rolled down my cheek and fell to the floor. Another one hit me in the chest. I looked to the back of the streetcar. Pete was there, smiling at me, holding another penny in his hand, taking aim. I walked to the back of the car and sat next to him.

Amy and her friends got off at the next stop without looking back to find me.

Pete and I rode together farther uptown, the streetcar humming and bucking all the way up the line. Pete said he'd been meaning to get in touch with me, but things had been so busy since he'd found a place to stay. The woman he was living with was really cool, he said, even though she was twenty years older. He was sure she could help me find a job and a place to live. He asked if I still had his little survival guide, and I wondered if he knew I'd looked inside.

"I'm sorry I bailed on you," he said, "but it was too good a deal to pass up. Evelyn didn't even want any money up front, she said I could owe her. And she knows everyone. She even lets me borrow the car. She thinks I have a license."

When we got inside their little house, Evelyn was serving dinner to her boyfriend, a sixty-year-old Cajun named Jacques. She got extra plates for the two of us and ran back and forth to the kitchen, bringing rice, sautéed shrimp, and peppers. When he thought Jacques wasn't listening, Pete told me, "She's a different woman when he's around. Totally subservient, but I kind of admire that.''

"Been to the parades?" Jacques asked. His voice was like gravel. "How'd you make out?"

We showed him our collection of beads and cups. Jacques was impressed.

After dinner, Evelyn rolled everyone a joint, and while Pete did the dishes—Jacques reminded him it was his turn—Evelyn showed me around. She showed me the corrugated metal vest she wore to play in Jacques' band and her collection of *Dark Shadows* videos.

"All the original episodes," she said.

Pete and I loaded some cups and a bottle of vodka into my backpack. The backpack had been a gift from the runaway daughter who had taken my place back in Portland. On the night she returned—the night before I left—we had stayed up all night talking while her mother slept peacefully in the next room. The girl spoke as if there were things she had figured out on the road, although she didn't name them, and we talked about her mother and other adults, using the word *adults* as if I wasn't one myself. She gave me the backpack, saying, "I won't be needing it anymore." We didn't talk of it, but I'm sure we both must have been thinking of our situation—of one kind of runaway displacing another.

Pete and I figured we'd drink and wander the streets all night, but it had begun to rain again. We stood for a while beneath a tiny awning, our backs pressed against the outside of a building. We could feel the paint chipping off the wall behind us, and I was thinking how, no matter where you were, a night in New Orleans was like a walk through a cemetery.

"I think I'm going to head back to the hostel," I said. Sometimes it was difficult coming in late. I wondered if Evelyn or Jacques would be waiting up for Pete. It was hard not to be jealous. He had his own little temporary family.

Pete didn't say anything.

"You can keep the pack with you," I said. I figured he wanted the alcohol.

"I'll give it back to you next time," he said. "You still have my book."

"Yeah," I said.

We nodded at each other, and I ducked out into the rain.

Whenever I ran into Pete on the street, or called him from a pay phone, he'd scold me for thinking I needed to look for work or an apartment on my own. "Evelyn knows everyone," he told me. "She can find us something." He said "us" as if I was included in this plan, as if he needed to take care of me, but the most he ever did when I asked about finding a job was tell me

I didn't need to worry. We'd buy food or a bottle with what was left of my credit, and Pete would give me a little of what was left of his food-stamp supply.

One night, Evelyn loaded us up in the car like a good mom would and dropped us off at Tipitina's with bottles of her Erotic Body Oil to give the cops outside in exchange for their letting us in free. Pete disappeared into the mosh pit immediately; I stayed on the side. Later, when he asked why I hadn't joined him, I said, "I guess I was afraid I might get hurt," and Pete said, "I hear you get that way when you're older."

Some days I would call to talk to Pete, and Evelyn would answer and say, "He's busy." Or, "We're just watching TV." And I knew they were probably fucking. I imagined it to the theme from *Dark Shadows*.

On days when Evelyn was gone, Pete would invite me over. We'd sit at the kitchen table and smoke the pot she kept in a large cookie tin on the table. The pot was cut thick, in big lumpy strands like my father's pipe tobacco, and never seemed to have much effect on me. I wanted to float, but there I was sitting at Evelyn's table, listening to Pete, who when he was stoned would talk in long sentences that seemed to last for hours. I'd just listen, becoming even quieter.

"Why do you let me go on like this?" Pete would say, and then he'd continue.

Pete was always talking about Kona, where he lived with his brother for two years. He told me about how they would do mushrooms and play in waterfalls and how they would survive on eating in hotels and writing false room numbers on the bill. "My brother said we'd never get caught," he said. "I know what it's like to trust someone and find out you shouldn't."

Pete stretched his arm across the table and pointed at me. He reached over and put his finger on the tiny scar beneath my left eye. He ran his finger gently over it, the only place he ever touched me.

"How did you get this?" he asked. "Did someone do this to you?"

I'd finally reached the level of numbness I'd been hoping for. I watched the gas flame that burned in the wall behind him.

"Never mind," he said. "You don't have to tell me."

Later Pete asked me, "Have you ever had a relationship with someone who didn't do something bad to your face?"

"Do you mean that literally?" I asked, even though I knew what he meant. "Or figuratively?"

"Either," he said. "Or both."

I thought for a moment before answering. "No, I guess I haven't."

. . .

When I finally found an apartment—signing the lease on a break between afternoon and evening parades—the landlady tried to talk me out of it. "You'd be better off in the Marigny," she said. "The crime there doesn't take you by surprise." The apartment was uptown, off St. Charles, in the midst of that sweet smell but overlooking a cemetery everyone seemed to have forgotten. Pete came by to check the place out, worried, it seemed, that I'd done something on my own. From my stoop, I watched him walk from the streetcar three blocks away, past the fenced-in yards and the bunches of green bananas that hung from trees just out of reach. Neither of us waved at first, as if we each thought we might pretend we didn't know each other. When he was finally too close for me to ignore, he raised his arm in the air, tentatively. I opened my palm toward him but kept it to my side.

The gas man was there, too, hooking up my line. Pete walked around the apartment, checking out the walls, the large ceiling fan that hung low enough to be dangerous to a tall person, the small roof deck outside the kitchen, and the crucifix someone had left propped on the mantel of what had once been a fireplace.

"Not bad," Pete said. "You can afford this?"

"Once my unemployment comes through," I said. "And I'm going to start looking for a job."

"Me, too," Pete said, but I didn't believe him. He didn't mention getting Evelyn's help this time, and I wondered if he had given up on that idea.

"I'm going to go to Kinko's to put together a résumé," I said. "Want to go?"

"After Mardi Gras," he said. "I'll go with you."

He looked around the empty apartment again. "You need a TV," he said. "I should steal you one."

I didn't know what to say. No one had ever offered to steal an appliance for me, but I didn't really have any use for one. The gas man looked up from what he was doing. His eyes moved from Pete to me and back again.

"If I had Evelyn's car, I'd do it for you," Pete said.

While the gas man was checking a connection in the kitchen, Pete lit the gas heater with his lighter. A flame shot up and died back down again.

"You shouldn't have done that," the gas man said. "You have to be careful with these things. It was about a year ago some kids like you died in their sleep. Carbon monoxide. In fact, I think it was this block."

After the gas man left, Pete said, "That guy's an asshole," as if the man was someone I needed to be protected from, as if the man's warning had been some kind of threat. There was a naive charm in the way Pete thought he might take care of me when he hadn't managed to do such a good job on himself.

There was no furniture, so we sat on the floor against opposite walls—as far from each other as we could get in my small apartment. I cooked some ramen on the stove and brought it over to him in a plastic bowl.

"I should have brought your backpack," he said.

"I don't really need it," I said, thinking I'd never see him again.

On his way out the door, he turned to me and said, "Hey, let's make plans. If we don't run into each other on Mardi Gras, let's meet the next day at the Please-U."

I spent Mardi Gras day thinking about calling Pete and hoping I might run into Amy; maybe her friends had left town and she'd be alone now and I could take her somewhere and hold her hand. I only had two dollars, but that was enough to buy a sixteen-ounce beer from a guy with a keg in the back of his pickup truck. I thought I saw Pete for a moment, but I lost him in the crowds of people wearing masks so it was hard to tell if you knew them or not. Most of the people wore masks that covered just around their eyes, so they still had a face, but it was hard to tell exactly what kind of face it might be. It was like there were three classes of people: the ones on the balconies promising beads to the people below them, the people on the street willing to do anything to get their attention, and people like me who just stood on the side and watched. I only wanted the day to be over so I could get on with my life. I walked through Jackson Square and up over the banks of the river to think again about my résumé and what kind of job I wanted.

The next day I sat in Kaldi's watching Mardi Gras refugees line up to use the pay phones, to call home and tell someone they wouldn't be returning as soon as they had planned. Old Billie Holiday records played on the loud speakers, and I liked the way she sounded in such a large, empty space. I kept thinking maybe I'd see Amy, and I called Pete to make sure he was still planning to meet me, but there wasn't any answer.

The pulsing of the streetcar made my head hurt. I got out at the Please-U Restaurant and took a seat in one of the booths. I laid Pete's survival guide on the table next to my place mat. The waitress eyed me suspiciously. "I'm meeting someone," I said. The waitress looked at me like she wasn't so sure. The other tables were occupied by men in suits, talking business as if, through some warp in time, the past few weeks of Carnival had never happened. At a corner booth, a group of nuns sat tallying profits from Mardi Gras beer sales.

I called Pete again from the pay phone. Evelyn answered. She sounded distracted, like she'd rather be somewhere else and somehow I'd interrupted.

"He doesn't live here anymore," she said, as if everyone knew, when she and I were probably the only two people who cared.

"Really? Where is he?" I asked.

"Probably somewhere in Texas by now," she said. "Look, I'm napping. Can we talk about this later?"

"Sure," I said, but I hung up knowing I'd never call again. I sat down at my empty table and for a moment imagined him crossing the flat Texas landscape, looking out at the big sky, his arm resting on my backpack at his side. I pictured Pete driving across Texas with someone more fun than me behind the wheel. And I wondered if he might have stayed if I had trusted him.

When the waitress returned, I ordered a muffaletta without worrying about the fact that I wouldn't be able to pay.

The place mats at the Please-U looked old and yellowed, like a decade ago someone had offered them a deal on a lifetime supply and they were never going to run out. I figured the horoscopes were so old, they probably told what had happened a long time ago rather than what to expect. I knew enough about my past. I flipped the place mat over, and in the blank space on the back, I wrote out two résumés side by side.

I wrote one for the kind of life I wanted and one for the kind I was likely to get.

things you can make
something out of

David needs *the report tomorrow at ten.*

Your sister called about dinner.

The sitter wants to know when to expect you.

We're still taking messages for Sarah, even though we know now that she isn't just late coming back from lunch. She's dead. Her car hit by an empty school bus, empty except for the driver. Hit at an intersection she shouldn't have been passing through, except that someone remembers Sarah said something about running errands, picking out new carpet for the office, picking up tickets for the vacation she'll never take.

Now Janice and Edie and I are pacing back and forth on the old carpet, taking turns at the phones, taking messages that won't be returned.

"She's still at lunch?" a voice on the phone asks. "It must be nice."

"Yeah," I say.

"Well, don't you want to take a message?" the voice asks. "Will she be getting back to me today?"

So I take another message, and pace my way out to the

veranda for another cigarette. I remember Sarah telling me, "If you don't stop that, it'll kill you," and me always promising to quit, thinking every time that I was telling the truth. Did I say anything at all to Sarah today? All I can remember is sticking my head in the office and seeing her busy on the typewriter, with that don't-talk-to-me-now-even-if-it's-an-emergency look on her face. It must have been a purchase order she'd been typing out—in quadruplicate—or she would have been at the computer. It can wait till later, I thought, whatever it was I was going to ask her. After lunch.

Then, when she was late coming back, Janice and Edie and I all noticed it, like we'd never noticed it on any other day when she was late. We all had something we wanted to talk to her about. We were all finding ways of wasting time, pretending to work at our desks but each of us waiting to ask her something— *Have you reviewed the résumés? Where's the McGlaughlin file? Has there been any work on the budget?*—things we needed to know before she left on her vacation. Loitering at files, lingering in front of vacant computer screens, we stopped doing our work, knowing that each time the elevator door opened it had to be her.

Then the call. Edie on the phone, Janice and I eavesdropping like we'd never do on any other day but knowing somehow that today was different. Edie covering the receiver to say, "Someone from the hospital wanting Sarah's husband's number." Edie not even being able to make a sentence of it. Edie saying, "Some kind of accident."

Just an accident. Maybe she'll need a ride back from the hospital. Who would go? All of us knowing everything would be okay, going on with pretending to work, me not saying the only thing on my mind. Why ask us for her number? Why not ask her?

Phone calls started coming. More than any other day. Everyone wanting to talk to no one but Sarah.

"She hasn't gotten back from lunch," I said.

I told Edie to call the hospital. See what was happening. "Shouldn't she be back by now?" All of us gathered around the phone. Edie put on her best phone voice—the one that commands respect without asking for it. Edie's blank stare. The hand with the phone in it dropping to the desk.

Edie saying, "Sarah was killed," and nothing more.

The phone calls.

She's still at lunch. She hasn't gotten back.

"Will she be getting back to me today?"

"I don't think so."

"Well, then, what about tomorrow?"

Pink messages for Sarah, piling up, waiting to be returned.

. . .

When I step back in from the veranda, Janice and Edie are waiting for me. The rival secretaries, who usually wouldn't be found on the same side of the office let alone standing side by side, are now standing next to each other, blocking my way.

"What are we going to do?" Edie asks. "Keep taking messages for the rest of our lives?"

"I don't know what to tell people," Janice says. "I feel guilty."

"I can't take the pressure," Edie says. "I'm about to snap."

"I'll tell them," I say.

I don't want to use the phone, so I walk from office to office delivering the news. I begin to feel guilty for taking people by surprise, watching their faces empty. Everyone moves in slow motion. They look up from their desks and smile briefly before the smiles fade and they wait for me to say something they already know they don't want to hear. I watch something invisible slip from beneath their faces, like a soul leaving the body.

It's Barb's last day. She's just cleared the last of her things from her office when I catch her walking down the hall. She's holding a box of framed photos and the crazy backward clock that only she can read—things that made her office hers.

"What is it?" she says.

I can't tell her. Barb puts her box down and reaches out to me, puts her hand on my shoulder. "Sarah's dead," I say.

"No, she isn't," Barb says. She's smiling. She thinks it's a joke.

"Sarah's dead," I say.

"No," Barb says. She shakes her head at me and steps away.

"Sarah's dead," I say. Barb leans against the wall and slides down to the floor. She becomes a ball at my feet.

Barb says, "I was supposed to go with her, but I canceled."

Janice and Edie and I go out for drinks when the day finally ends. Janice and Edie wait in the hall while I gather all the pink messages for Sarah from our desks and shuffle them together in a neat pile on Sarah's desk. *Lunch tomorrow? . . . I have the information you needed. . . . Call before you leave; I want to see you.* I look at the photos of her children lining the desk—I may have met them once at a party—and the framed degree on the wall. A master's in acting, she had decided, was impractical once she had children.

We go to the same bar we went to the first Friday after I started work. There was time to talk then, that first day, Sarah playing one of her games for everyone to get to know one another. Me feeling awkward, the only man in the group. All of us going around the table, giving nonsense answers to serious questions.

What's the most painful thing? someone asked.

I said something stupid, like locking your own hand in the car door—the hand with the keys. I didn't tell anyone I'd actually done it. By the time we got around to Janice, we were already up to "A proctologist with long finger nails." Then Sarah said, "Knowing that you've broken someone's heart," and gave no explanation. It seemed so melodramatic, none of us could think of anything to say. It was one of those things you file away, waiting for a private moment or long car pool, to ask.

I never asked.

None of us are talking much today. Just drinking.

Janice says, "I keep thinking . . ."

"I know," I say, not wanting her to say it out loud.

She's thinking of the times we went out drinking because we didn't have anyone to go home to . . . and to complain about Sarah. To plan our imaginary coup of the office. We knew there was no way Sarah would leave on her own.

"We need some kind of accident," Edie would say.

I drive out to the art-supply store, still buzzed from drinking, expecting to be killed. I'm always saying I'm going to be an artist. I'm just working this job till something happens. But I always put off working on it. Nothing I do has to do with art. At work Sarah would say, "You're the *artist*," every time we needed a flyer or design. It made me cringe because I knew she didn't believe me.

I walk past the aisles of paper and glue and paint and scissors. Things you can make something out of. I finally settle on this little black portfolio, a sheet of foam, folded and closed with a couple of buttons. It probably cost eighty-nine cents to make. I pay twenty-five dollars. Now it's sitting on the passenger side of my car, the side of Sarah's car that was hit by the school bus. It's sitting on the seat next to me, and I'm thinking, "What can I do with this?" I keep looking through the passenger window to see if anything is approaching.

Sarah took me on a shopping trip when I first arrived. Was there talk then, in the office, of something between us? But it was a just a little shopping trip. The best places for produce, the best place for meat, the best of everything at the best price. I didn't have the heart to tell her that what I usually eat comes in a box and gets cooked in the microwave. Lean Cuisine. Stouffer's. Maybe even Chef Boyardee. So I loaded up on flour and sugar and cans and vegetables, and I told myself I'd learn how to make something out of them. But it wasn't that easy.

Easier to use the microwave. Let someone else do the hard work for you.

• • •

In the morning we pass around the paper. Sarah's car crushed in the photo on the front page. Proof that it's true. No one talks much. There's nothing to say. We just retreat behind our cubicles. I can hear the sound of Kleenex being dispensed on the other side. Somebody's posted a sign-up sheet. Volunteers to make dinner for Sarah's children. I sign my name on the list and wonder whether I can patch several frozen dinners together into one casserole.

A conversation we had just days ago. It may have been our last conversation face-to-face, we spoke so often by phone, even within the same office. Sarah and I were talking schedules, meetings, setting goals for the day.

"I hit a bird on the way to work today," I told her, not thinking, not stopping myself from saying something that didn't seem to belong. "It was a pheasant, I think, and it was just standing in the road staring at me. I tried to slow down, but it was too late. Then it tried to fly away, but it just hovered in the air in front of the car. Thudded against the windshield. I pulled over to look for it, to see if it was okay, but there was just a cloud of feathers in the air. No trace."

Neither of us said anything. We were just staring at each other, both of us thinking the same thing, wanting one of us to explain why I'd just said that and not wanting to know. Just staring at each other for a second or less, the kind of second that seems like something more.

At the memorial service, a juggler performs, which seems kind of contrived. And he isn't very good. He keeps stumbling, dropping the balls, wandering around the stage trying to regain control. Janice and Edie and I keep looking at one another from the corners of our eyes, trying to see if we're the only ones who don't know what to make of it. Actually, the entire crowd is doing the same thing. No one's watching the juggler anymore. Everyone's watching each other, trying to make sense of it.

I remember the dream I had last night. The one about religion. It was all deep colors, air filtered with incense, and cold, cold as stone. It was like a Madonna video without the sex; it was endless.

During the sermon I keep my eye on what's beneath the cloth on the altar. Even though I know it's not true, I keep expecting the preacher to dramatically lift the cloth to reveal an urn. "This was Sarah," he will say. It will be so dramatic, I'll find it impossible not to laugh. But of course I'm wrong. When he lifts the cloth, it is Communion.

I stay in my seat, because I've never taken it. It looks easy, but I might make a mistake. I might gag on the host or drink too much of the wine. I watch Edie and Janice sipping from the chalice, and I think about the three of us drinking on Friday afternoons, with nothing better to do than plan accidents we never really hoped would happen.

When it's finally over, no one says anything, but you can tell we're all relieved. No one talks about the juggler. A memorial service isn't like a movie or a play. You can't turn to the person next to you and say, "I don't know, I just didn't get it," or, "I was disappointed, how about you?"

Or, "The life was better."

At the reception, people mill about in tiers. At the center of the room, Sarah's husband, her family, her closest friends. Edie and Janice and I stand in the outer ring, just watching, not talking.

Some people, like Barb, aren't here at all. I haven't seen her since she collapsed in the hall, her box of belongings resting sideways, things spilling out onto the floor. Barb's gone now, too; we'll never see her again.

•   •   •

Sitting at her desk, I'm thinking it's Sarah's desk and I shouldn't be here. It's Sarah's papers I'm trying to make sense of, her papers stuffed into my new black portfolio on her desk. It's her black leather chair I'm sitting in. Her books on the shelves—I wonder which she had read and which she was planning on getting to. Sarah's kids in the plastic frame on the desk: a boy and a girl; they look like they must still be in grade school, but how old are the pictures? The new carpet she ordered is rolled up in the corner, waiting to be rolled out once we get rid of Sarah's things. How embarrassing it will be when she catches me sitting here. I'll have to explain how silly it was to think she was dead. How upset people will be at me for lying and saying she was dead. A ridiculous lie. What was I thinking?

If she were here, she'd be able to make sense of it and it would all seem simple. "Just pick up the phone and make the calls," she'd say. "Tell them the truth. It will all fall into place."

Janice and Edie are back at work in the next room, back on opposite sides of the office, as if everything has returned to normal.

The calendar on her desk says, "Sarah out," and there's an arrow drawn through the next two weeks. Her vacation.

We were trying to schedule interviews before she left. We were looking for Barb's replacement. The deadline was tight. I asked Sarah, "What should we do while you're gone?"

She said, "You'll just have to go on without me."

I pull a pink message from the pile and reach for the phone.

. . .

At home in my kitchen, I fit six frozen casseroles into one pan and slip it into the microwave. Swanson. Stouffer's. Lean Cuisine. Ore-Ida. Beef Pot Pie, Spinach Soufflé, Mac and Cheese, Lasagna. I carve away the sides to make them fit neatly. I make up my own formula for how to cook it. I add up all the cooking times and divide the total by one and a third. While it cooks, I keep one eye on the oven window and rout through the drawers looking for toothpicks, crayon, construction paper. I label sections with tiny banners, like flags for foreign countries, although the borders have melted together and it is hard to tell where one ends and another begins.

I wrap the casserole in the brown paper bag the ingredients came in. Rest it in the passenger seat and head down the road, hoping it's secure.

Mary had begun worrying about the amount of time she spent thinking of her own pangs of paranoia. Worse: she wondered if other people had picked up on these concerns and, if they had, what might they be saying about her when she wasn't listening? Not that she'd been around any other people in the past several days—the exceptions being the denizens of Tompkins Square, where she went for an occasional walk. Not that anyone there had a clue to who she was. She had just moved into a sublet in the neighborhood, into the apartment, actually, of a woman who had baby-sat Mary when they had both been significantly younger.

Coincidence? Mary wondered. Or someone's idea of a good deed, a staged but reassuring random act of housing? Perhaps her parents had paid the woman off. Wouldn't she be the laughingstock when word got out?

Not that there was anyone here who knew her, not that if word got out, anyone would really care.

Mary wondered for a moment if it was possible. It had been her mother who called with the offer, telling her that Lisa was going back to Africa again and was looking for someone to take care of her place while she was gone. "But you might not want to," her mother had said. "You know that neighborhood is a little dangerous." Mary didn't think of the Lower East Side as a dangerous place. She'd gotten used to living in dangerous neighborhoods and actually had grown to prefer them, because the people mind their own business and nothing bad that happens ever takes you by surprise.

She'd spent the last part of the summer staying with Shannon and Kim in their new home in Westchester. Her staying with them had been sort of an accident. She had meant only to visit, driving up after spending a few months in New Orleans, before deciding what she might do next. She had posted a sign in a coffeehouse in the French Quarter, RIDE OFFERED. TO ANY-WHERE, because she didn't know where she wanted to go, only that she wanted to go somewhere. The first person to call was looking for a ride to New York. Mary thought, as long as she didn't get out of her car in the city, there was no chance of running into John. But since Shannon and Kim had this new place in the country, Mary decided she might as well stop by after dropping the guy off in Manhattan, even though she knew Shannon was her best friend only by default.

. . .

But on the way up to Westchester, driving along a particularly curvy stretch of the Hutch, Mary had one of her little mishaps.

Mary's was a one-car accident, except for the guy who slowed down as he passed the wreckage and shouted from his window, "I'll call the police!" She had packed everything loosely, just tossing things into the car, so that after the accident, everything was strewn, lunaticlike, from the dashboard to the back window. Old clothes, paperbacks, notebooks, commemorative cups from McDonald's and Mardi Gras. The inside of the car looked like one of those arcade games, where you operate a little crane that digs through plastic treasure. While she waited for the police, she sifted through the remains, taking only the things that seemed important.

When the police arrived, Mary was holding only three things and was staring at the star shape her head had made in the windshield.

The policeman took one look at the car and said, "You must be drunk."

"It was an accident," Mary said.

"How did it happen?"

"I was driving and then there was a crash."

"You have to be drunk," he said. He walked over to what used to be the guardrail and pointed to the post that her car had pulled out of the ground. "Six feet deep they put these, so things like this aren't supposed to happen."

He held a pen in front of her face and asked her to follow it without moving her head. "Well," he said, "you just failed that test, so you must be drunk."

Mary couldn't remember the last time she'd had a drink. It had been months ago, before New Orleans, where alcohol was so available she felt no desire to have it. "Maybe it's because I just cracked my head with the windshield," she said. She meant it the other way around.

He said, "No, that wouldn't affect you."

Curious people pulled over to watch. The officer left Mary at the side of the road and took statements from them to include in his report. Then he came back to her and said, "It smells like your battery is leaking." Mary wasn't sure what he wanted her to do about it, so she didn't do anything at all.

The EMTs arrived, took one look at the car, and promptly taped Mary to a board. When they asked if she wanted to go to the hospital, Mary said she wasn't sure. They asked if she knew who the President was. Mary couldn't stop laughing. They told her she was probably okay but she'd have to sign a form if she didn't want them to take her with them.

Then Mary started to tell them about John and how the last time she was in New York he had punched her in the face because of a story she had written about their dysfunctional relationship, which he thought had portrayed him in a bad light, and how everyone thought her nose was broken because it had bled so much, so she went to the emergency room and they said everything was fine but they charged her six hundred dollars for this, and that except for John, whom she hadn't spoken to, and the bill, which she hadn't paid, everything turned out all right because she used to have these chronic nosebleeds but she hadn't had a single one since. She started to tell them this, but she caught herself midway through.

"I just can't afford to go to the hospital," she said.

They shoved a clipboard in front of her face. The form said something about how if she ended up paralyzed from the neck down, they couldn't be blamed. She thought of her parents caring for her all their lives; it was an idea that was both welcoming and frightening. "Then I guess I should go," she said.

She wouldn't have been able to sign it anyway. They'd already taped down her hands.

Later, in a coffee shop on Avenue A, she told a stranger what it was like as they carried her into the back of the ambulance, how she thought to herself, this must be what it's like when you die. And how later, in the emergency room, it was like one of those movies where somebody wakes up dead but they don't even know it, so they end up wandering the earth for eternity wondering why none of their friends are talking to them. And how then Shannon showed up and said, "This is the best thing that could have happened to you."

At first Mary wasn't sure if Shannon was talking to her or to Kim, who was on the other end of the cellular phone that Shannon held permanently to her head. The cellular phone had been a gift from Kim to mark the anniversary of their pre-engagement. Mary thought of it as a form of house arrest. Then Shannon snapped the phone shut and said, "Mary, I want you to think of this as a new beginning," as if she was about to offer a cosmetic makeover. On the way out to Shannon's car, Mary was holding on to just three things: an envelope of pictures that had fallen from the glove compartment of her car, a paper plate with important phone numbers, and a collection of short stories she'd been reading on the trip.

Shannon said, "I guess I won't need to open the trunk."

"I left everything else behind," Mary said.

"Good," Shannon said. "You need to let go." Mary noticed that Shannon was holding Kim's phone over her heart, as if she was about to say some kind of pledge. "You can stay as long as you want, Kim and I have discussed it."

"Oh, it shouldn't be long," Mary said. "I just have to figure out what I'm doing with my life."

"What are the pictures of?" Shannon asked as they drove. She didn't notice Mary looking out the window for the spot where her car used to be.

"That trip John and I took." She and John had made up stories about how they were driving each other crazy and sent them on postcards to their friends. Later, it seemed like everything they said actually had been true.

"I think it's time to let go," Shannon said.

Mary said, "I think you should let go of that phone and put

both of your hands on the wheel." And looking out at the exit signs, she added, "You used to be upset with me for not being angry, then when I was angry, you told me I shouldn't be bitter, now that I'm not bitter . . ."

"I just don't see the point in remembering when you have a perfectly good opportunity to forget." Shannon said this with a big smile on her face, so she could claim it was a joke if it sounded bad.

When Mary and John were writing their postcards, Mary suggested he accuse her of being passive-aggressive. He didn't know what it meant. Mary told him it was what passive-aggressive people accused each other of in the middle of an argument about something else.

Almost all of the photographs in the pack were of trees, an entire roll of film John had taken from the car window as they passed; they all looked nearly identical, as if they had passed the same spot over and over again. And then, in the middle of the roll, there was a photo John had taken of his own reflection in the sideview mirror. He must have spent minutes adjusting the mirror and the camera angle, getting everything just right. Mary was sitting next to him and hadn't even noticed. It was that photograph Mary wanted to hold on to, not to remember him, but to remember that there had been things she'd been wrong in not paying attention to.

"It was just so stupid," Mary said. "I just don't want to forget how stupid it was."

"Was," Shannon said, raising an eyebrow. "*Was?*"

"Was."

Shannon reached into her purse and handed Mary a diet mint as a sort of reward.

Shannon and Kim had purchased the home not as a step toward marriage or commitment, but because Kim had insisted it would make a good investment. It had been owned previously by a young couple with two children, and they were able to negotiate a good price because the man's wife had been killed in an accident and he was anxious to get rid of it and move on. Shannon gave Mary a tour of the house, acting more as a real estate agent, selling her on the idea of living there. "Kim stays in the city a lot," she explained. "He kept his apartment. So there's plenty of room here."

"I really only need a little time." Mary thought the house was furnished all wrong to belong to friends of hers. Everything was large and sturdy, too heavy to be easily moved. Mary had spent the past year using floors as desks, sleeping in nests made of her own out-of-season clothing until she felt confident enough to invest in a bed; the problem was she never felt that confident, so she had learned how little a person really needs to survive.

Shannon showed her a large aquarium in the hall. It housed a single goldfish. "There were more," she said, "but they all died off while Kim and I argued about whose responsibility it was to feed them.''

With Kim in the city and Shannon at work, Mary had the place pretty much to herself. In the mornings she liked to pretend she was staying at some sort of fancy retreat, where she imagined a life that included only the people she wanted in it, if only she could figure out who they might be. In the afternoons she took field trips, looking for signs of life. About a mile's walk away, she found a run-down university, occupying what used to be a farm. It was a sort of holding tank for young urban refugees, kids from Brooklyn and Queens who had to get out of their parents' house but didn't know where to go. Mary watched them wandering the campus at midday, having nothing more important to do than blow off the day's classes. It was as if they had a license she was lacking: permission to do nothing. A tunnel running the length of the campus was a mine of graffiti. Mary walked through it several times a week, as if it were a local museum. Some of the graffiti was top-notch and seemed to hold a sort of historical significance. Beneath the surface of paint, you could sometimes see another image bleeding through. And it was there, beneath the flaking paint of newer work, that she first saw it again—that annoying doodle of John's, a locomotive with cockroach legs. He'd scribbled it on her ankle while she slept, the first night they were together. Later she realized he scribbled it everywhere.

When she wasn't out sightseeing, she was on the phone with

the insurance people and her credit-card companies, asking them if they could just wait until the insurance money came through. The AmEx lady spoke to her as if she was her closest friend. She said, "I'd like to help you, but you're too great a risk."

Mary began to develop a fondness for the goldfish, whom she named Hank because she couldn't remember ever having known someone with that name and she thought maybe that was the person she was waiting for. Hank remained aloof, loitering around the empty ceramic castle, looking in the windows as if he expected someone else to be there.

"Why don't you call a friend," Shannon suggested. "Invite them up for the weekend."

"Like a slumber party?" Mary said. "I don't think so." Mary didn't want to see anyone from the past. She didn't want to have to explain how she'd spent years moving around and going nowhere, while they stayed in one place and got something done.

"I know what you mean," Shannon told her. "It's like me slaving away in the office and finding out John's making a fortune selling those T-shirts in the lot next to Tower Records."

"He is?"

"Oh . . . no. I was just being hypothetical."

. . .

When the insurance money arrived, Mary realized there were times when even Shannon could be right. Maybe the accident *was* the best thing that could have happened to her. The settlement was four thousand dollars and change. Enough to buy a new car if that's what she wanted, but what Mary wanted was never to get in another car again. She could pay off her bills and still have enough money left to put a deposit on an apartment.

She called the AmEx lady to tell her the good news but found out the bill was already in collection. "And good luck finding a place to live with your credit history," the AmEx lady said.

When she realized it was true, it would be impossible to get something on her own, Mary spent a weekend interviewing for shares in Brooklyn. Shannon said that when she called Kim and told him what Mary was doing, he said, "I didn't realize Brooklyn had gone public."

"Funny," Mary said.

Shannon said, "The scary thing is, I don't think he was joking."

What he was probably thinking, but not saying, was that with Mary gone, he might actually feel obligated to move in.

The first house she visited had four floors, six bedrooms, three baths, two kitchens, and a very competitive atmosphere. They'd invited about thirty candidates to an informal reception, which began with a short presentation by the four remaining roommates, followed by the declaration: "Let the schmoozing begin!" The second focused their discussion on the merits of Gilbert and Sullivan. The third was concerned with Mary's cleaning habits. "What brands do you use?" they asked. It had been so long since she'd had anything to clean, she couldn't think of an answer.

So by the time Mary's mother called with the offer of an apartment on the Lower East Side, Mary was willing to accept something that otherwise might have struck her as too easy. The train into the city reminded Mary of the streetcar in New Orleans, of days spent riding uptown to the library on St. Charles and then back into the Quarter to find a good table to spend the rest of the day.

Mary's baby-sitter was packed and ready to leave by the time Mary arrived. She handed over the keys and led her on a quick tour of the neighborhood, showing her the spots to know and those to avoid. She showed her how the bodegas on Second Avenue were more expensive than those on Third, how just down the street there was a spot where everyone went if they were looking for something to OD on, and how farther down there was a place that offered free acupuncture as a form of recovery. Then she walked Mary farther west, to the health club where she'd arranged to have her membership transferred to Mary's name from her own. That's where she kissed Mary goodbye, wished her luck, and disappeared into a cab heading uptown.

It was that first night in her new apartment that the phone

calls began, late at night, hang-ups, as if someone was calling just to see if someone was home.

The following day in the health club, Mary ran several miles on a treadmill, watching how the other women all seemed to have personal trainers, someone they paid money to to stand next to them and tell them what to do. And on the treadmill directly across from her was a woman wearing a T-shirt with a design that looked familiar to her. A locomotive with cockroach legs. Or was it the other way around? It was hard to tell which way it was changing. Mary remembered John scribbling it on a bar napkin once, while she was hiding in the bathroom. When she had come back out and asked him what it meant, he'd said he couldn't tell her, as if it was too personal.

Mary still couldn't tell what it meant. But across the bottom of the shirt, beneath the design, he had written PROGRESS?

Looking across the room at the woman and her T-shirt, Mary thought it was a good thing they were running on conveyer belts. Otherwise, they would have run right into each other.

It was at Nobody Beats the Wiz, in front of a bank of televisions playing the opening credits of *The Mary Tyler Moore Show,* that Mary saw John again for the last time. She had been window-shopping for the furniture she didn't need to buy, pretending she was furnishing a new apartment. She'd spent the afternoon in boutiques filled with the essential downtown items: folding furniture, CD racks, halogen lamps, clever shelving units. She felt a secret relief in knowing she didn't have to buy anything, having gotten her apartment entirely prefab. In one store, she stood staring at a small dining table constructed out of odd black tubes that held themselves together through tension. She and John had had this table, and she'd taken half of it with her when she left and then let it be towed away with the wreckage of her car.

"You like?" the salesman asked when he spotted her eyeing it.

"No," she said before leaving. "Not at all."

She was standing before the bank of televisions, watching the credits of The Mary Tyler Moore Show, thinking how every week they stopped with her hat still dangling in the air, just as she was about to catch it. Or drop it. It was hard to tell which way it would go. It was then that she had her epiphany, that Mary Tyler Moore's character actually progressed from episode to episode. She got promotions. She got a raise. She moved to a new apartment. It occurred to her that this was unusual for a television character. It made the character different from anyone she knew in life.

She spotted John over in the telephone section, kneeling on the carpet, checking out the phones. For a moment it felt like spotting a celebrity, the adrenaline rush of it, and then the disappointment when you realize you don't care. He was exactly as she remembered him. The same black leather jacket. The same pale skin. Only his hair had gotten a little longer and nattier. His face looked puffy. He didn't look good. John kept lifting the receivers to his ear and then resting them back down again, as if he was expecting someone to be there.

Mary had never realized how much she would want to kill him, and how practical the decision might seem. She walked across the room and stood over him. He seemed so small to her, so inconsequential. She could just reach down and pop his head off, like a dandelion. He didn't even know she was there. He was too busy lifting the empty phones to his ear and resting them back down again in their cradles.

A salesman approached Mary and asked if she needed his assistance. She shook her head no and walked back to the televisions, where the *Mary Tyler Moore* episode had begun; she was trying to give another party. Mary realized her heart was pounding. She was experiencing an adrenaline rush. She'd read about these things, how in a crisis people find themselves capable of superhuman strength. In a few minutes, if he was smart, John would be gone, and she would never see him again. And then she would spend years wondering what might have happened if she had gotten close enough. Mary walked away from the televisions and back over to John. She said his name aloud.

"I'm surprised you would speak to me," John said.

"So am I."

"I'm buying a new phone."

"Yes."

They stood for a moment, wondering what to do. Mary heard a voice say, "I'm really sorry about everything that happened," and realized it was her own.

"It's water under the . . ." John waved his hand in the air, as if he was trying to brush away a cliché. He said it as if she had borrowed a book and forgotten to return it.

"I hope so," Mary said. She looked at the distance between them. Fighting distance. Both of them close enough to throw a punch and far enough to get out of the way.

John smiled, and his lips parted, as if there was something he was afraid to say.

Mary continued. "Because I was really worried about what would happen if we ever ran into each other again."

His smile faded. He didn't speak. Mary wondered what he might do if there weren't people around. Was he suppressing the urge to give her a good punch, the way he had the last time they ran into each other unexpectedly? She wondered if he might go home now and tell people he'd seen her and she was doing really well, as if he'd had the courage to speak.

"Well, maybe we'll run into each other again," she repeated, hoping it wasn't true. He said nothing, and Mary realized that's what he was.

Out on the street, Mary wondered if she meant what she'd said about being sorry. She supposed it was true. She was sorry for what had happened, for thinking he was a different kind of person than he was. She looked over her shoulder and through the store window. John was back at the phones, lifting and resting.

Shannon and Kim were arguing in the kitchen when Mary arrived to get the last of her things. She hadn't expected anyone to be home at all and was rather annoyed at the distraction. They quieted down when she walked into the room, but Mary could see sweat beads forming on their brows.

"I saw John the other day," Mary said, desperate to fill the silence.

"You what?" Shannon said.

"Well, I didn't plan it. I just ran into him. It was an accident."

Shannon said, "I hope there was an apology involved."

"There was."

"Really?"

"Well," Mary said, "I told him I was sorry."

"You!" Shannon screamed. "What were you thinking? I would have cut off his balls."

Mary was surprised by this. Shannon was always claiming to be John's friend. "But I *am* sorry," Mary said.

Kim said, "That doesn't mean you should tell people."

Mary packed her things—which by now were few—into a

shopping bag and took the train into the city for one last time, after dropping a thirty-day feeder to Hank on her way out the door. He was still hanging out by the castle, looking in through the windows to see if anyone was there.

On the train home, Mary sat at the window watching the small towns arrive and disappear, arrive and disappear. She was suddenly reminded of New Orleans and of a guy named Jason she'd spent time with her first few days there. She really didn't spend *much* time with him and they rarely spoke, just shared an occasional cigarette in the courtyard of the hostel where they stayed, becoming familiar with each other's presence but neither venturing forth with anything real to share. But she loved to watch him from a distance, admiring how he knew how close he could get to people and how far to stay away. Then she lost track of him, until the day before she left, when she saw him walking up St. Charles, his hair tucked up in a cap, his head bobbing up and down to some interior music. The streetcar was stopped, and she was sitting in the rear of the car, on the empty engineer's seat that the tourists aren't smart enough to take. She watched Jason for a moment without realizing who he was, and then he looked up and across the distance between them and waved to her. She waved back, just as the streetcar began moving again. Jason began running, and for a moment Mary thought perhaps he wanted to talk to her. Perhaps he had something to say. She thought of getting off at the next stop and running across the street to wait for him on the corner.

But as she watched and the speed of the streetcar picked up, she decided against it. They were both moving in the same direction, but the distance between them remained the same.

She told herself it was an illusion. That they had nothing to do with each other. That it was impossible for her to tell if he was running toward something or away.

Or maybe just running.

like incest

1.

I still think of you every time I enter a service station, which may be why I avoid them, why I never drive anymore, why I prefer traveling in distances so great they require a plane, the vacuum of air travel, in which time doesn't seem present until you hit the ground. Although, if I'm not careful, it's that vacuum that will get me, the way everything we did together haunts me even though it exists in a vacuum, in a space that can't be reached, a space that seems to have no connection to what came before and after it. But that's probably what appealed to you at the time. I remember you; you like things that are temporary.

2.

Did you hear I totaled that car we rode in? That I had them tow it away with all my belongings—everything you knew about me—because I never wanted to see them again? I'd spare you the details if I saw you. You would find the situation contrived, the irony forced. I will not tell you that what I hit I didn't see coming. That I was blinded by the sun.

3.

I remember your face. I can trace it in the air with my hand. I watched it from the corner of my eye while you drove, past landscape, past exit signs we would contemplate and then avoid, choosing instead the straight line, the highway. You said, "Always forward, never back." You never liked to stay in one place long. When it was my turn to drive, you slept, and I watched you instead of the road, but when you were driving, I could never sleep, too busy watching. Watching you, watching the road, watching the things we passed and left behind. The passing lights sweeping across your face at night, reflecting green and blue from your skin.

4.

You caught me looking once. You said, "You don't trust me." I didn't say anything. Just kept watching, because I knew I'd be leaving you behind.

5.

It's that time of year again. New Year's. Snow pressed flat on the ground. We make pilgrimages to these little meccas, service stations with gas pylons, neon lit, outside. The attendants are our guides. The snow in the lot pressed into a surface so smooth, I can walk across it without leaving a print. Without a trace. Inside: fluorescent light, the coffee, plastic-wrapped snacks, *USA Today*. Things we can count on.

6.
Patsy Cline.

In Ohio, while you used the rest room, I paid for the gas. The woman eyed us suspiciously. Your leather jacket, I assumed. I bought a Patsy Cline tape, to make her feel at ease.

Sweet Dreams.
   Walkin' After Midnight.
   Crazy.
   I Fall to Pieces.

7.
You told me: "There's such a thing as consensual incest, you know." You were fishing for something in your bag and looked up to get my reaction. We'd been telling jokes, and you told the one about incest that didn't make me laugh.

. . .

"Of course there is." But I wondered what you meant by that. And at the same time, I didn't want to know.

8.

Remember Graceland scared me? Not the place itself, the shrine to Elvis, the jungle room, but the two of us there together, already off course. Of course you might not have known how it scared me. We'd agreed to come there—together we'd agreed that it was what we'd always wanted. To see Graceland. We wanted the same thing, and it scared me.

You, of course, probably didn't notice at all. You were busy in the reflection of the mirror, checking your hair, choosing the right glasses, adjusting your lipstick. Your admiration of smooth surfaces. And that morning I noticed for the first time how you took hours in the motel bathroom, just to get ready to get back into the car.

I think we were both disappointed. It wasn't as tacky as we had hoped. A guide explained the mirrors that covered the walls. "That was done to create the effect of enlarging the small rooms." I thought it had the effect of making a crowded room seem twice as crowded. Everywhere I turned, I saw myself surrounded by strangers.

. . .

You began to take my picture there. In front of the mansion stairs, holding my plastic souvenir cup. A piece of me, that picture, you could hold on to when I was gone. I wondered what you saw through the lens. In those pictures of me. Something I couldn't see myself? I think of the Indians, who believe a camera will steal their souls, and I think you could have stolen mine. I would have let you. If I was sure that I had one.

Would you let me take a picture of you?

9.

"What's the strangest thing you've ever done?"

It must have been me who asked it so casually.

You said, "I stole a cat's heart."

"I stole a cat's heart," you said calmly, your eyes still on the road ahead of you. "We were dissecting cats in high school, and I stole its heart. I dried it out and carried it in my purse. I guess I felt guilty because I don't even like cats. So I carried it with me. Then I got tired of it and I threw it away."

. . .

I told you how I like cats, because they are quiet and keep to themselves and still manage to get whatever they want. I told you how in high school we didn't do cats, we did worms. We sliced them right down the middle and pinned them open on wax trays. And then we were tested on their anatomy. They're all strings inside. I couldn't tell anything apart. The teacher asked me to point to its heart. I pointed generally at the whole thing. He gave me an A.

10.

Sometimes you would speak of him. Of how you had to leave. How you came to realize there was a surface to him beyond which you could never reach. You never spoke of loving him, though. You worked your way carefully around that one.

And remember what you said to me one morning, after you rose from my bed?

"I have no feelings for you," you said.

I told you, "Who said anything about feelings?"

We looked through each other. It was hard to tell which of us was the better liar.

11.

Then we drove to New Orleans, and we slept together there. In the morning, on your way out of the bathroom, you assured me, "I don't remember anything that happened last night," as if you had willed it away.

And I lied, too. I said, "That's okay. There wasn't much to remember."

12.

We arrived at the Voodoo Museum a few minutes late for the tour. The main altar is covered with photographs that have been pinned above the mantel. Some are old and tattered, black and white, others are new, Polaroids that look as if they were taken days ago. I wanted to ask, "What do they mean? Who left them here?" but it seemed private. These private photographs on public display.

Our guide was a dark-skinned woman wrapped in bright cotton cloth and carrying a purse, a heavy bag, as if she was in a hurry to get somewhere else and this tour she is guiding was just a brief stop she's obliged to make. She stumbled over her words. She explained that she isn't the voodoo queen, that the voodoo queen died recently of an aneurysm, on the anniversary of her father's death.

You whispered, "Like incest," and then moved through the crowd, looking at the statues of snakes, the drawings of a naked woman dancing in the forest with a snake held high above her head. You stopped in front of two glass cases in the corner and you looked inside.

The woman was speaking about the balance of good and evil, how they don't exist separately because they are all part of the one. She was saying we need to allow these things to flow rather than holding back.

You told me I should look inside. All I could see at first was my own reflection in the glass. Then I saw the snake coiled in the case, staring me in the eye. The snake flicked its tongue at me, and I took a step back.

I heard you asking, "What does the snake mean?"

The woman stumbled on her words again. Saying, at first, it means nothing. Then, when pressed, saying it is a symbol of what we hold inside.

Later, you said, "That woman didn't know very much."

13.

How many days did we spend there? I don't remember, except that it was more than we should have. And that we had to speed across Texas afterward to make up for lost time. (Did you know I moved back there, to New Orleans, for a time? Just like you always said you wanted to.)

Every morning, we called for our horoscopes, thinking the service was free, not realizing there would later be a charge. I remember mine said I'd be spending time with a nasty loved one. Could that have been you? And yours said that something you were hoping for would come true. I remember thinking it might have something to do with me. Which was silly.

In front of the hat shop on Dauphine, we stopped and looked at our reflections in the window.

"I've always wanted one of those," I said.

You told me, "Then you should have one."

What I was looking at—remember—was a harlequin hat, the hat of the fool. The kind of thing I'd always wanted the freedom to wear but felt a little too self-conscious about. Frivolous. But you told me I should have what I wanted, so I bought it. Then you complained about the bells ringing from the tip of the hat, jingling every time I moved the bag.

14.

You always wanted us to drink too much, so we wouldn't have to remember. One night, on the way back to our hotel, you pulled me into a courtyard and pointed up at a statue, a tower made of poles intersecting one another in hexagrams. You said, "Do you realize there is no reason this should be standing? There's nothing holding the pieces together, just the tension between them." You wanted to play on the bars as if they were a jungle gym. I just wanted to go home and get into bed. I thought of how you would be returning from this trip, how everything was waiting for you back home just as you left it. But I would continue on.

I wanted to trade places with you that night.

15.

We crossed Texas, the big sky. Endless blue. You were hanging out the window, playing with the camera, taking pictures of the flat landscape as it passed. You said the sky wasn't really blue, that it was an illusion, that you knew this was true because your brother had told you and he had heard it from a teacher at school.

. . .

"Blue doesn't really exist. We see it as blue, but as a pigment it doesn't really exist."

"That doesn't make sense," I said.

16.

We should take more back roads, I thought. So there we were driving up the New Mexico desert in the middle of the night. We hadn't counted on so many miles of nothing. We hadn't thought the desert at night would be so cold. So flat that all the earth was below us. It looked as if we could fall across the horizon.

You slept next to me. I tried to stay awake, weaving across the road in the fog, in and out of the headlights of oncoming trucks.

I pulled to the side and stepped outside. I walked to the edge of the road and stared out across the snow-covered desert. I could hear the sounds of trucks somewhere beyond the horizon.

"Are you okay?" you called out from the window.

"I just want to stay here," I said, but not loud enough for you to hear.

It is so quiet here.

17.

We visited your friend Liyana, in the mountains above Taos. She was living with her parents then. I got a card from her last month. She wondered if I ever heard anything from you.

Their house was one large circular room. The floor was made from packed mud. The family sat in different sections of the house and could speak to one another without raising their voices. They could hear every sound.

When I needed to use the bathroom, I followed your footprints in the snow to the lean-to in the back. A wooden platform and a lid, a bucket of hay where you would expect to find paper.

You went on and on about how everyone should live this way. And then, later, you said, "I don't know how they can stand it."

I was too busy thinking about Liyana, and how, when we asked if she was happy out here, she said, "No. I'm going back."

18.

We pulled into a service station to use the rest rooms. Another couple pulled in next to us and rolled down their window. They must have been surprised to see another couple out so far.

. . .

"Where are you going?" they asked.

You replied, "Nowhere."

They laughed and gave us their number. "Call when you get there."

19.

We made one last stop in Needles, although we could have driven straight through to L.A. and ended the trip a day sooner. You said, "We have a bottle of tequila to finish," and I agreed. Then we sat at the little table in our motel room, and we argued all night.

I said you were mad at me because I wasn't getting drunk enough to forget what might happen.

You flicked your tongue at me, and I said, "You remind me of a snake when you've been drinking."

You didn't say anything. I said, "Or maybe you remind me of a snake when I've been drinking."

You said, "I don't have any feelings for you." There was a sort of forced laugh beneath your words.

. . .

I said, "I never said anything about feelings."

And then you locked yourself in the bathroom for the rest of the night.

20.

We didn't know the La Brea Tar Pits are closed on Mondays. It was too late, we'd already found a spot to park. We walked around the outside of the buildings, around the chain-link fence. The sky, I remember, was a mix of clouds and smog and blue— that blue you told me doesn't exist in life. I remember this, the way I remember photographs you took, even when I never saw them.

The rain had made the tar pits overflow, beyond the fences and over the sidewalks. We had to walk carefully around the edges.

You were looking for a statue of a cavewoman. You stepped around a corner ahead of me and turned back shaking your head. "Nothing."

I asked, "Didn't the Flintstones have an episode where they visited the La Brea Tar Pits?"

"Probably," you said.

. . .

"But isn't that strange? Like they were visiting the site of their own demise. Like tourists. Like they already knew their fate but were completely detached from it."

"Yeah," you said. "But it was just a cartoon."

You were staring into the distance, toward the statues of two mammoths. One was sinking desperately in the tar, while her mate was standing on the shore, struggling to pull her out.

"It looks like she's moving," you said.

I told you it was just the wind.

21.

You kept asking me, "Have you called your friends in San Francisco?" I thought what you meant was that you wanted me to leave. So in the morning I packed my things and called Ondine.

She asked, "Is everything okay there?"

I said, "I just want to get on with my life," which sounded true, but I realize now that what I felt was the opposite. I just wanted to stay there with you.

. . .

I sat on the edge of the bed and woke you. The first words you said, before opening your eyes, were "I'm sorry."

I said, "I'm leaving."

You acted as if the whole thing was planned this way. You said, "Wait a minute while I go to the bathroom." I sat waiting, wondering what it was you were doing in there. Wondering if it was too late to change my mind.

You followed me out to the car and watched as I started the engine. I remember being surprised that neither of us was saying good-bye. I rolled down the window and stuck out my hand. You held it for a while.

"Well," I said. "I'm glad you came along."

"It was an experience," you said.

And then we let each other go, and I thought of the sculpture you showed me in New Orleans and the tension that held us together.

22.

I remember you, staring at your own reflection in a hotel mirror, checking your appearance, to see if anything shows.

23.

The joker's hat, the Graceland cup, the postcards and maps, the number of the people we were supposed to call from nowhere when we got there. I had them towed away.

I wonder what happened to the photographs you took.

24.

And yesterday I met a man in a coffee shop. He said he was visiting from L.A. We spoke for a while about the places we had been. He stretched his arm across the table, laid his hand palm up, and I saw he had written on it a list of five things he needed to do, errands to run, phone calls waiting to be returned. Your name was third.

25.

I wonder if he reached you.

Mary takes her time doing her side work—filling the salt and pepper shakers—just so she can watch him. Kevin moves like a dancer: head up, squatting to pick things up, cocking his head slightly to look for something, stretching his arm out to grab, his weight on one leg, keeping the rest of his body in line. Kevin is the kind of man Mary's always been fascinated by, so alien, so remote. The kind of person you have to travel to, even if you're in the same room. And once she reaches the tiny psychic space these guys occupy, she thinks, this really is an isolated spot, isn't it? But there's a safety there, too.

All of Mary and Kevin's dates so far have been safe ones. In fact, they haven't really been dates at all, working late together and heading out for a nightcap—something nonalcoholic for Kevin—so it didn't seem like spending time together, just an extension of their commitment to be part of the same work team. And then, the other night, she caught herself—too late—saying, "I was going to call you last night, but I changed my mind."

"I was thinking of calling you, too," Kevin said. "I decided to wait, since we were getting together anyway. I decided to preserve the energy, you know.''

"We need to pace ourselves," Mary agreed. She'd already had a sense that this thing with Kevin, whatever it was, was something that would dwindle rather than grow. She watched him swing open the door to the bar, one hand on the door, one foot on the ground, his head turned toward her. She didn't want to talk to him, she thought. She just wanted to watch him.

Even alone, he nods his head for emphasis, as if he's engaged in conversation with an invisible partner. Lately he's acknowledged to himself that the ongoing conversation in his head is mostly about love. He wonders if he's capable of it, because to love or be loved requires a loss of balance. Kevin's life has always seemed to be guarded by issues, and this new one—balance—is the latest. It certainly wasn't an issue when he was drinking—not just the loss of physical balance then, the falling down, but also the chemical imbalance, the cycle of alcohol sandwiched with nicotine followed by greasy food at an all-night diner. And when he was drunk, there was no telling what else he might try—it was the perfect excuse—so he worked himself up from simple intoxication to the more complex. Pot when cigarettes were unavailable, a little coke when his stamina was lagging.

Once, he'd tried heroin, letting a stranger shoot him up in the bathroom of some downtown club. He'd thought it was the most extreme thing he could do, the pinnacle of his downward slide— that's why he'd done it, to finish things off, let the cycle peak.

But it was too easy. He wanted more.

And that's when he stopped, working his way backward through his habits, drinking only occasionally and then not at all.

He found he missed the connection he thought he shared. The sense of community he felt in a room of drunks with the music too loud to talk; or seeing someone on the street and knowing they'd once drunk from the same glass. He tried AA meetings but found the people too desperate, attributing success to a higher power and failure to themselves. So he spent a lot of time at home, sitting in his apartment, fine-tuning the list of foods he could eat. He'd been feeling sleepy, napping a lot. He was trying a diet made almost exclusively of protein: eggs and tuna, the occasional bean. He felt better but suspected the effects would soon wear off.

The last time he'd had sex, it was with a woman named Sharon whom he'd met in a local coffee bar. While they fooled around on his futon, he listened to his stereo change from disc to disc and thought, "Wow, this is lasting pretty long." Kevin was the kind of man who measured relationships not in months or years, but in number of songs. Afterward, they said to each other, "That was pretty good," and "That was intense," as though they'd forgotten it was supposed to be that way. He thought of describing it as a "peak" experience, but he worried it would scare her away.

They exchanged phone numbers, but neither called.

There had been a time when Mary thought things with Kevin might actually go somewhere, but the relationship she had proposed in her mind had gone quietly sour soon after the beginning, without any mitigating factors, without any stormy arguments; they hadn't even gotten that far. The momentum had dropped out. Mary hadn't been able to pinpoint exactly when, but the center seemed to have spun out from under them.

She thought perhaps she'd been expecting too much. She'd been known to do that.

Activities were suggested—movies, theater, an exhibit or two—but never confirmed. Coffee dates were missed alternately by one or the other. Subway construction was blamed.

And then Kevin said, "Hey, you know, I've been feeling some tension in my neck, in my jaw, and I was going to go, you know, get some needles . . . in my ears . . . acupuncture. I thought maybe you'd want to come along."

Of course, this was a lie. There was no tension. Kevin had been following a self-prescribed regimen—megadoses of Motrin and melatonin—in an effort to attain a sustained but unnatural state of bliss.

And Mary knew this was the case, but she said, "Yeah, sure," anyway, because the treatment was at this free acupuncture clinic—the Harm Reduction Center—and the idea sort of scared her. It gave her a buzz the kind of which she hadn't had in a while, and she could tell herself it was her curiosity about the place that brought her there, rather than her curiosity about Kevin.

But the motivation behind Kevin's invitation hadn't been entirely pure; in fact, it hadn't been entirely inspired by Mary. He'd been thinking of someone else, of Natalie, and it had been Natalie who first took Kevin to the Harm Reduction Center on the Lower East Side, before she replaced Kevin and acupuncture with visits to the other needle clinic—the Needle Exchange—followed by a trip to the ATM, to the Spot, and back to her apartment, where she sat at the edge of a tub filled with cool water, hoping that if she OD'd, her fall into the water would revive her in time to call an ambulance for herself.

The Harm Reduction Center was run by the same people who started the Needle Exchange, but it was free massage and acupuncture they gave out, to help people better deal with their addictions. To replace one form of dependency with another. The trouble was, it was real close to the Spot, which was always open for business, so on days when the HRC opened late, clients came in already high on dope, and with acupuncture on top of that, they ended up immobile in the corner of the room—human pincushions propped up in heavy chairs like they were waiting to get their hair done.

"It's not the same needles," Natalie told him before his first time at the clinic.

But Kevin wondered why not. And: Did people really *exchange* needles at the Needle Exchange? He wasn't sure, but if they did, why not wash them up and use them again? Why not use them for acupuncture?

There was a long ramp that ran down from the entrance from the street, as if people might be wheeled in and out, although Kevin had never seen this happen. The lounge area, where this healing was administered, was surrounded by black scrims meant to reduce the outside light, but light shone through the space between each panel, more distracting than if there had been no scrims at all. A small box produced the artificial sound of the surf but was often drowned out by arguments passing on the street outside.

His first visit at the center, he watched an older woman— skin, translucent, hanging from her bones—as she plucked the needles from her ears and dropped them into a receptacle marked HAZARDOUS WASTE.

Natalie handed Kevin a swab for each ear and whispered to
him about the woman who was waiting to stick them. "She's a
needle freak," Natalie said. "She loves needles. Heroin, acupuncture, body piercing, tattoos. When it's slow in here, she
sits in the corner knitting."

It hurt more than Kevin expected, the woman sticking five
needles in each ear, each at a slightly different angle. He looked
over at Natalie's ears, the needles sticking out of them, following
the curve, the bell shape of her ear. He remembered pinning
butterflies to cardboard when he was young; he did it because
they were beautiful.

"You're snoring," Natalie said. "It's time to go."

An hour had passed without Kevin realizing it. He looked
over at Natalie. His head felt loose. There was a dizzy fog in his
mind, and he liked it.

"You shouldn't do more than an hour," Natalie said.
"You'll end up worse than when you came." Natalie began to
pull the pins from her ears. A trickle of blood ran down one
ear.

"You've got some blood," the needle lady said. "That's
good. It means we hit a level we haven't reached before."

Outside, on the street, Kevin felt like a dog with its head stuck
out the window. Natalie was so afraid of losing him, she had to

reach behind and grab his wrist, leading him back toward the subway uptown.

"Are you all right?" she asked. "Are you going to be able to find your way home?"

Kevin nodded. "I'm fine," he said. "Don't worry about me." But he knew he was lying.

Just before she turned away, back to her own apartment, he added, "I really had fun with you today."

"You were asleep," she said.

He wandered recklessly toward his apartment, seventy blocks uptown, stopping only for a sandwich and then to throw the sandwich bag away without remembering that he had stuck his apartment keys in the bag for safekeeping. He was too busy careening, dreaming up the names of women he might ask to have acupuncture with him when Natalie wasn't around. Which led him eventually to Mary.

At the Harm Reduction Center, her first time there, Mary stared across the room at a woman who looked fifty but was probably in her twenties. You could see it in her eyes, she was young, but the body looked as if it belonged to someone else: her mother. This woman was chatting up the paunchy man next to her, both of them engaged in frantic conversation with needles sticking out of their ears, shouting at each other as if the distance between them was greater than it actually was.

"Your friend shoots porn?" the woman was asking. "I've done porn. I can show you my pictures. You can give them to your friend. I need some cash. I do anything."

This is supposed to be relaxing? Mary thought. In the back, someone was burning incense. Mary was allergic, but she was afraid to say anything.

"Don't cross your legs," the woman suddenly advised her. "It throws things off balance."

Mary looked over at Kevin. His lids were resting at half-mast. In his right hand he was gripping what she didn't know was a *new* set of keys to his apartment. She imagined this was what he would look like in a morgue. It was like one of those true-crime photos where the eyes are painted open after a violent death.

"Want to leave?" Kevin asked.

He stood next to her at the mirror and showed her how to remove the pins. She reached over to swab his ear.

She said, "You're bleeding."

Outside, they considered stopping for coffee, but Mary was distracted by a fortune-teller's window.

"I think I need a fortune today," she told Kevin.

"Go ahead, get one."

As Mary approached the door, the fortune-teller rose to greet her. She looked out at Kevin and asked, "Are you together?"

"No," Mary said.

The fortune-teller led her by the hand and shut the door behind her. Kevin stood watching for a moment through the glass, but when Mary turned again to look at him, he was gone, and she realized she had answered wrong. They *were* together.

"You have too many needy people in your life," the fortune-teller said. "They come to you with their problems because you listen to them. You need to stop listening to others and think . . . no, listen . . . for yourself."

The woman sounded like Oprah. Mary couldn't believe she'd just spent fifteen dollars to be told something anyone could have told her. She'd wanted facts, not common sense. She thought about the desperation of the woman getting acupuncture, offering her services to anyone who would listen. Did this woman have a family? Did anyone care?

What happens if no one loves you? Mary wondered. Do you just disappear?

Kevin was up the street when Mary found him, outside a deli, drinking coffee from a blue and white paper cup.

"So, what did she tell you?"

"That I spend time with the wrong kinds of people. Nothing I didn't know already." She immediately wanted to apologize, but it was too late, and she didn't want to sound insincere.

Kevin barely seemed to notice. He'd been thinking about Natalie. About her call the night before. Her apology for not keeping in touch, but she'd been in the hospital again. She'd overestimated how much she could take—two packets was more than enough. And she'd decided to be sensible about it, to snort it rather than injecting it or smoking. She'd divided it out in small lines and decided she could have one every hour. One every half hour. One every fifteen minutes.

And then it was too late. She could feel herself sinking and called for help.

"It's that scholarship," she said. "Now that I don't have to work, I have too much time to fill. I'm afraid to go outside."

"Read a book," Kevin suggested.

"Okay, I'll go to the bookstore," Natalie said.

"No! I'll bring you one." He was worried what might happen if she ever went outside. There were a million bad opportunities between her and the nearest bookstore.

"Hey," Mary said as they were walking. "You're really out of it."

"No," Kevin said. "I was just thinking about something I have to do."

"Oh." Mary wondered if he would tell her, or if he was playing coy and waiting for her to ask. She let him walk ahead a few steps so she could watch him, and Kevin let her follow him without telling her where they were going. It hadn't been such a good date after all, he thought. He could tell she hadn't enjoyed it, but he was at a loss for any solution to fix it.

"Come on," he said, holding open the door of a bookstore. "I have to look for something, and then we can get a cappuccino."

Mary said, "Okay," even though she was beginning to feel she was in the way. In the bookstore she felt suddenly obsolete, out of place, out of date, stale, as if she was about to be remaindered. Kevin was busy moving through the aisles. He wouldn't tell her what he was looking for. He lifted the books, read the covers, returned them to their spot on the shelves. He wanted to find something that struck a balance; everything seemed either too happy or too sad. He wanted to give Natalie something that would make her happy but something she could believe in as well, and books with happy endings seemed unbelievable to Kevin. The realistic books worried him because they offered no hope.

"What's that?" he asked Mary. She was holding a thin paperback in her hand.

"It's a sort of modern romance, I guess," she said, surprised to be suddenly included. "I think I read it last summer."

"How does it end?"

"I think they end up together, sort of . . ."

He worried for a moment that if he gave the book to Natalie, she might take it the wrong way. She might just call him and launch into a cynical rant about the uselessness of romance and ask him what was he thinking.

"You know," Mary said, handing him the book, "sometimes it happens that way."

And Kevin took it from her, thinking maybe it was worth the risk.

But will he move closer to her? she wonders now, as she sits filling salt and pepper shakers in the darkened corner of the restaurant where they work. Or will he move farther away?

happy people

On New Year's Eve, Ruth and her husband went to a late matinee of a Woody Allen film in a theater on the Champs-Élysées. Ruth remembered that the film had received rather unflattering reviews back in the States, but seeing it here added a special sort of cachet. Besides, they had grown tired of walking, and it was good to sit down. The seats were big and cushioned, and they even reclined and rocked back and forth a bit. They didn't have seats like these in the theaters back home.

When the film was finished, Ruth turned to her husband and said, "I think the subtitles made it better, don't you?" Neither of them spoke French, so Ruth found the lines written at the bottom of the screen added a sense of mystery the film otherwise lacked. She wondered if they really said what she was hearing in English, but she liked the fact that she would never find out.

Her husband didn't answer. He didn't care to travel. He was content to stay at home with her, to wait for the children to return on visits from college, but he had recently come into some money and had told her she could have whatever she wanted.

Earlier in the day they had called the children, who were at home on a break between semesters. They had called just to see how they were doing. The truth was, Ruth wasn't worried about them as much as she missed them. Spending the holidays abroad had seemed a romantic idea, but now she felt it was a shame to be away during the one part of the year when she ever got to see them. Ruth had forgotten which way the time zones ran and had woken them in the middle of the night. "Are you all right?" they asked her. "Is everything okay?"

"Don't lose yourselves," she said, the way she always did talking to them long-distance on the phone. And her children always agreed, even though they were too young still to know what it was she was saying.

After breakfast they had taken the Métro to the outskirts of town, to Porte de la Villette, where an old slaughterhouse had been converted into a high-tech museum. It wasn't the kind of thing Ruth particularly cared for, but she thought her husband might enjoy it more than the Musée de Pain. Ruth hoped they might go there, too, before they left. A museum of bread. She found the idea very comforting, though she couldn't imagine how they might fill an entire building with bread artifacts. But the French, she was certain, could find a way. The whole city was filled with the most unlikely things, and everything seemed

to have once been something else. And then there was the Pom-
pidou Center, the entire thing built inside out.

But they were at Porte de la Villette, in the Cité des Sciences
et de l'Industrie, in an exhibit on the senses. There were black-
ened rooms you could walk into, and you knew where you were
simply by the sounds coming out of the speakers. A concert hall.
A crowded cafe. In another room there were large plates, like
satellite dishes, placed at opposite ends of the room. Stairs led
up to the center of each dish, and if you whispered into the dish,
the sound traveled over the heads of the crowd to the person at
the opposite dish. Ruth spoke to her husband that way for several
minutes, the two of them whispering back and forth across the
crowded room.

They returned to the Hôtel Select for a nap in the afternoon.
They slept opposite each other in small twin beds. Ruth woke
first and watched her husband sleep. She had spent most of her
life expecting very little, because there were times, when she
was young, when she'd expected too much—and from all the
wrong people. Even in college, at a dance, spotting a man she
might like, she would step away rather than toward him. She
might be husbandless, she thought, if she hadn't taken a trip one
weekend to visit a friend, if she hadn't ended up at a party in a
school where she knew no one and, seeing him standing against

the opposite wall, walked over, taken his hand, introduced herself, the way she imagined a man would, thinking there was nothing to lose, she'd never see him again, she was leaving the next day. How happy she was to have made such a mistake.

She didn't want to wake him, so she sat reading the hotel literature, comparing paragraphs in English with their French equivalent, trying to decide which words corresponded with each other. According to the brochure, Eric Sevareid had stayed there as a young journalist, paying just twenty-five cents a night. Now it cost over a hundred dollars. Ruth remembered having watched him on the news, always reporting from some chaotic scene that in those days seemed unimaginably far away. Then suddenly he was retired. She hadn't even noticed him getting old.

They hadn't counted on the restaurants being booked with New Year's parties (it didn't seem a holiday without friends and family there), so they wandered the streets of the Latin Quarter looking for anything that might take them in. They found a Chinese restaurant on rue Saint-Jacques. Mirama. Ruth wondered what the name might mean but didn't ask.

"It doesn't seem right to be eating Chinese in Paris, does it?" she asked her husband, who laughed and held open the door.

They were seated at a table near the front. Ruth looked past the glazed ducks hanging in the window and watched as the crowds grew thick out on the street. Four students with back-packs pressed their faces against the glass to look inside. Two girls, two boys. Ruth thought they were Americans. For a moment she met the gaze of one of the boys, and she wondered what he was thinking of her. He was wearing his jacket inside out; Ruth wondered if that was the style. He reminded her of her own kids, who were probably getting ready to throw a party she didn't want to know about, or maybe the clock ran differently and they were already cleaning up, discarding empty liquor bottles, scrubbing stains from the carpet. She wondered where these kids' parents were, and after they left the window, she wondered if she should have invited them inside.

She would remember to write another postcard to her children when they got back to the hotel that night.

At the end of the meal, the waiter offered fortune cookies in a variety of languages. English, French, Italian, and German.

Ruth asked if she could have one of each. The waiter smiled and brought back two sets—one in a bag for her to take home. She cracked open the cookies one by one and spread the fortunes out on the table, wondering what they said. First the German, then the French, then the Italian. She handed the last one to her husband and told him to keep it a secret.

They walked down Saint-Michel to see if Shakespeare and Company was still open. Ruth thought it might be nice to read a book. They browsed the tables looking for something light. She realized there were a lot of English authors she hadn't heard of before, and even the ones she knew were unrecognizable in their British editions. The covers were different, and the quotes on the back were from people whose work she didn't know. Her husband handed her a book, a collection of stories she'd remembered reading about. Ruth paged through the stories.

"He doesn't write about happy people, does he?" she asked.

Her husband replaced the book carefully on the shelf.

In the square of Saint-Michel, people had begun swimming in the fountain and climbing to the top of the statue, perching on its shoulder, trying to remove the sword it held over its head. Strangers wandered the square, kissing each other and throwing empty champagne bottles into a large pile of shattered green glass in the middle of the street. Ruth worried that someone might be hurt. It was impossible to move, but they made their way slowly back toward their hotel, passing liquor stores lined with empty shelves. Ruth heard two American men telling a German girl that they had just come over that day and would be leaving in the morning. Was it possible that people did things like that?

An elderly woman passed and kissed them both on the cheek. Without thinking, Ruth returned the kiss. It wasn't until the woman had moved on that Ruth realized she was homeless. Ruth couldn't imagine kissing a woman like that on the streets back home.

A fight broke out ahead of them, and the crowd moved out of its way, clogging the path even more. As they inched their way farther, Ruth thought she recognized one of the boys who had been watching them through the restaurant window. He was surrounded by a gang of thin teenagers with shaved heads. They were taking turns beating him. Ruth's husband pulled her away before she could be sure if it was him.

They began to lose their way in the crowd, missing the turn to the Hôtel Select and continuing up the street, toward Saint-Germain, where from a distance things seemed to be calm. As they reached the corner, another couple turned down the street toward them, leaning into each other for drunken support as they walked. Just as quickly as they had appeared, they lost their balance. Ruth watched as they fell against a discount-store window, which shattered beneath their weight and fell on top of them in triangular shards. They lay still in the display box, next to the mannequins, as if they were sleeping, a blanket of glass draped over them for warmth.

Ruth and her husband ran over together without saying a word. The man began emerging, rising to his feet, dusting himself off, and once he had regained his composure, he wandered away, leaving the woman behind, as if nothing had happened. Ruth dropped to her knees and began to lift the glass off the woman's body, one piece at a time. She could hear the woman moaning. When she had removed all but the tiniest of pieces, her husband lifted the hysterical woman to her feet. Ruth saw the uniformed legs of a police officer standing next to them. She looked up to the woman's face and saw that there were small cuts around her face and she was crying.

Ruth rose to her feet and reached out to take the woman's hand. Ruth's hand slipped easily, absently, into the woman's coat sleeve, which hung loose at the end. Her finger's searched instinctively for other fingers, for the palm of the trembling woman's hand. But there was nothing there to hold on to. The woman's arm ended at the wrist. Ruth drew back and then saw that she hadn't lost the hand just then—there hadn't been one there to lose. Looking at the woman's lipsticked grimace, the cuts and blood on her face, the dusting of glass that covered her winter coat, and yet the woman's drunken calm, Ruth felt sick with the knowledge that this wasn't the worst that had ever happened.

Then Ruth felt her husband take hold of her and whisper, "Come on. I'll take you home."

For a moment, she'd forgotten he was there.

acknowledgments

Thanks to everyone, but particularly to Jenifer Berman, Jill Bossert, Peter Christopher, Lucille Clifton, Nathan Douglas, Jennifer Egan, Phil and Lisa Evans, my family, David Gilmour (and Liz Duncan), Rebecca Goldstein, Kevin Grivois, David Groves, A. M. Homes, Maureen Howard, Suzanne Jordan, Laura Josephs, Neva Knott, Sheila Kohler, Daniel Lanois, Alex Lucas, Aimee Mann, Jan Meissner, Ellen Miller, Rick Moody, Candace and the Mulligans, Michael Murphy, Ben Neihart, Tom Paine, Susan Perry, Sam Phillips, Lisa Queen, Alice Quinn, Yariv Rabinovich, Sharyn Rosenblum, Paige St. John, Joe Salvatore, Luc Sante, Ben Schafer, Helen Schulman, the Sewanee Writers' Conference, Dani Shapiro, Tom Spanbauer, Laurie Stone, Rebecca Sudul, Betsy Sussler, Catherine Texier, Ann Treistman, Andes Van Syckle, Suzy Vitello, Rob Weisbach, The Writer's Voice, and the Corporation of Yaddo.